F*ck, Really? Sexploits, Facts & Fantasy 2.024

Dr Emma Goodall

Contents

1

Foreword

This book is meant to be both helpful and entertaining. If you find something particularly interesting, share it with the person or people you are having or want to be having sex with.

Written in an open and non-judgemental manner, sexual scenarios and stories from a range of people are followed by guidance on relevant conversations and actions needed to ensure this can be explored in a safe, sane and consensual manner.

The author has written sex and relationship education curricula in Australia as well as a sex and relationship book for teenagers and young adults. This is a very different style book, for adults.

2

Background

This book came about because I finally got around to it, after years of my friends asking me to please do a sex and relationships book for adults, rather than just teenagers.

All stories in this book are de-identified true stories, shared with consent. The stories illustrate the points being made and can be read by themselves or along with the rest of the content. The stories start with icons such as:

icon

and the text is in this font.

Sexual acts, intimacy and playing are the terms used throughout this book to indicate the sexual interactions of two or more people, together, for the purposes of sexual pleasure and/or connection.

These can take place within a relationship, when dating, when in a situationship, FWBs (friends with benefits), or as fuck buddies as well as during a ONS (one night stand) or hook up.

This book aims to educate and entertain, so that people can identify and explore their sexual fantasies and desires without judgement, in their heads before going out into the 'real world'.

3

Safe, Sane and Consensual

All sexual acts or intimacy should be grounded in consent and be inherently safe and sane. That does not mean that acts of bondage or sado-masochism are deemed unsafe or insane if they leave marks. What is does mean is that the people involved need to be able to continue their lives without being physically broken and/or emotionally and/or psychologically messed up from the sexual acts.

Personally, I never engage in sexual acts unless I and they are sober, as in not drunk or not on drugs. This was not always the case, and I can sadly say from my own and others' experiences that playing whilst high and/or drunk, whilst it may seem a good idea at the time, often is not.

The BDSM community are particularly open about sex and that 'playing' needing to be safe, sane and consensual, but it applies to all relationships and sexual acts or intimacy. BDSM is the acronym for Bondage (using restraints of some kind), Discipline (power and control), Domination and Submission (asserting / giving power and control) and Sado-Masochism (pleasure from giving or receiving pain). BDSM sex and relationships are sometimes described as kinky, leading to the question; 'What are your kinks?'. Non-BDSM sex and relationships are often described as vanilla. However, there are a range of kinks and fetishes that fit into neither category.

For example, a foot fetish is a sexual desire that eroticises feet. This may be seen or described as kinky but is not necessarily a part

5

of BDSM, though it may be incorporated into it. Some kinks and fetishes can be explored and enjoyed alone, whilst others need another/others to be fully enjoyed.

Online can be a safe space to find others who share your kink/fetish as well as a very unsafe and predatory space. Be aware that anything you share online may be shared on to others without your consent, despite this being illegal in many parts of the world. Many people online are not who they say they are, and whilst this may be to keep themselves safe, it may also be to lure you into a false sense of security.

Relationships that are not safe, sane and consensual are abusive and unsafe. Saying you are into BDSM does not give you the right to beat someone up and rape them. These are illegal acts and have no place in a healthy world. Sadly, many people do not understand the myriad of rules and communication that need to be put into having a healthy BDSM interaction. If you meet someone who is interested in any kind of BDSM interactions with you and they do not ask about your limits, do not 'play' with them, as it will end badly.

If you are in an unsafe or unhealthy living situation, seek help and support from domestic/family violence agencies to leave safely. If you are in an unsafe or unhealthy relationship, it is wise to seek assistance and guidance on how to break up safely. Leaving is the most dangerous time in an abusive relationship, so please seek help to leave safely. Look up organisations from a public access computer or using an encrypted browser, so that your partner cannot find out that you are looking into how to leave.

Consent can be thought of as a spectrum from non-consensual to active affirmative consent. Kai Chen Thom referencing Betty Martin's work on consent, suggests that there are four parts to this spectrum of consent, with two being non-consenting and two consenting.

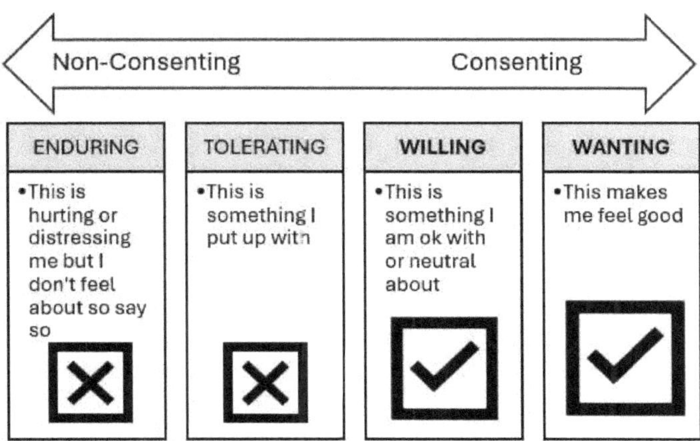

4 types of consent

In the healthiest of relationships, both/all people are wanting all the sexual activities and intimacy that takes place. However, during getting to know you and exploring phases of relationships, there may be a range of willing incorporated too.

Many people, of all genders report they both tolerate and endure sexual activities in both new and long-term relationships. This is often done because people are either being coerced, which is illegal in some places and unethical in all, or due to a misplaced sense of "I should be keeping my sexual partner happy, even if it distressing or unpleasant for me."

4

Language notes

Humans have so many different words for our body parts and the things that we do with them. This book is meant to be accessible and easy to read, so I have not used formal language unless necessary.

A vagina is called a range of different things including pussy, vaj, vjayjay and cunt. A penis is often referred to as a cock or dick. Some people even give their body parts names, such as 'little man' for their penis. Whatever you want to call things is fine, as long as you make sure not to offend someone you are intimate with, by calling their parts offensive names.

The following three images provide information around human biology, sexual anatomy and erogenous zones. Erogenous zones differ from person to person as the way we experience pleasure in individual. This image is for general rather than specific, accurate for all, information.

Human biology and sexual anatomy:

https://library.achievingthedream.org/herkimerbiologyofaging/chapter/

anatomy-and-physiology-of-the-male-reproductive-system/

cc license free to use and adapt

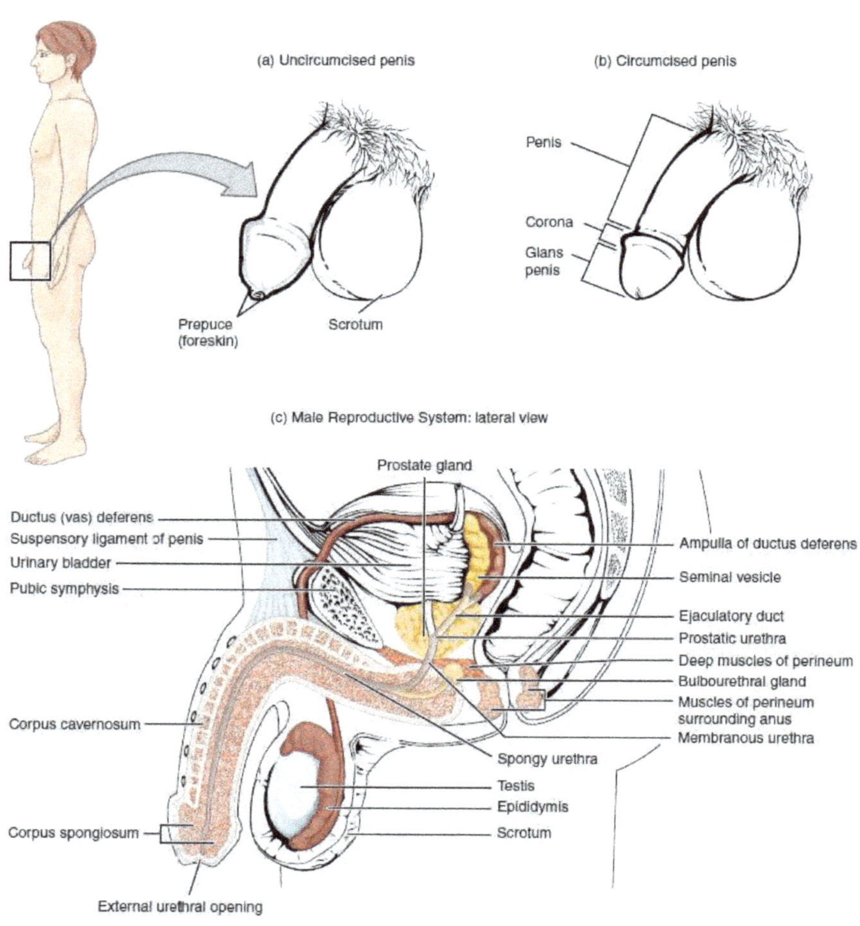

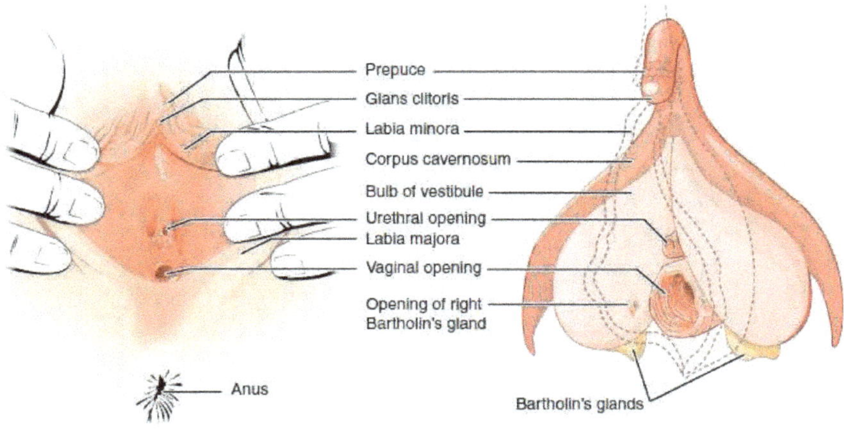

Vulva: External anterior view

Vulva: Internal anteriolateral view

https://library.achievingthedream.org/herkimerbiologyofaging/chapter/anatomy-and-physiology-of-the-fe-

male-reproductive-system/

cc license free to use and adapt

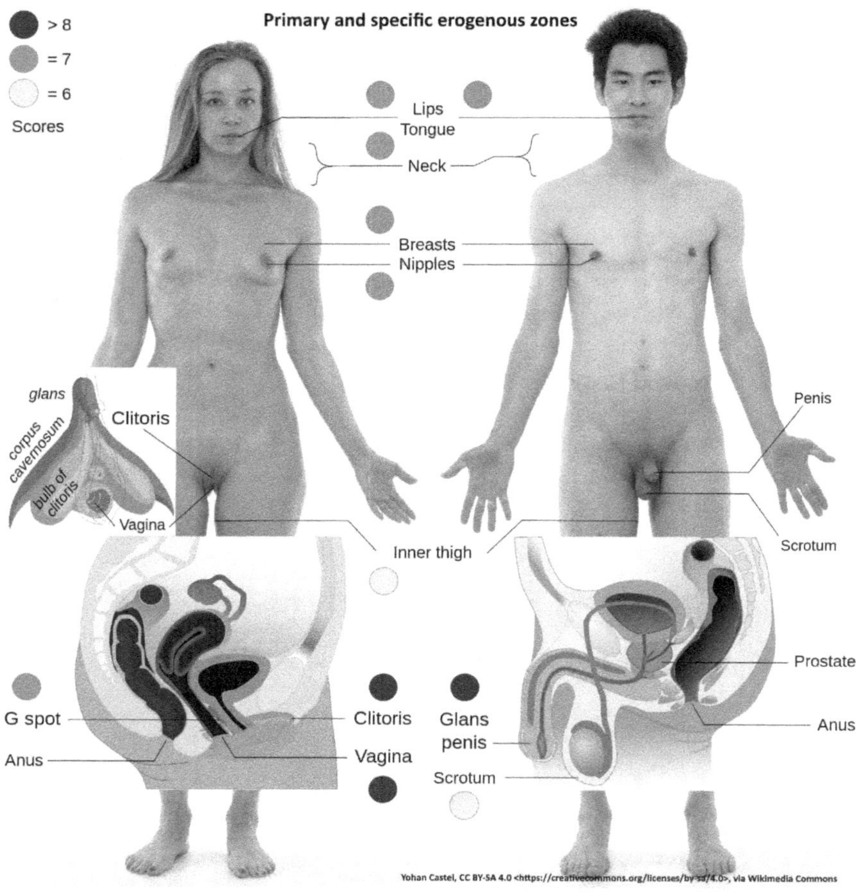

> 8
= 7
= 6
Scores
Primary and specific erogenous zones
Lips
Tongue
Neck
Breasts
Nipples
glans
corpus cavernosum
bulb of clitoris
Clitoris
Vagina
Inner thigh
Penis
Scrotum
G spot
Anus
Clitoris
Vagina
Glans penis
Scrotum
Prostate
Anus

5

Gender

It is sometimes assumed that gender is and always has been a binary, but this is not the case at all. There have always been more than 2 expressions of gender in use, particularly in indigenous communities around the world.

AFAB – assigned female at birth

AMAB – assigned male at birth

Cisgendered (cis) – a person whose gender identity is the same as the gender identity assigned at birth

Transgendered (trans) – a person whose gender identity differs to the gender identity assigned at birth

Gender expression and identity are often understood to be social constructs, with what it means to be a man/male or a woman/female or non-binary/gender fluid, gender queer etc being different in different cultures.

Sex on the other hand refers to an individual's biological status as viewed through the lens of their external anatomy. Sex is typically assigned at birth as either female/woman, male/man or intersex. Intersex refers to an individual with biological differences and reproductive anatomy that does not fit the typical definitions of female or male.

Masculine and feminine are aspects of gender expression or identity that take place within the context of place and space. Expressions may be through hairstyles, clothing, use of voice etc. What is seen to be masculine and what is seen to be feminine is often determined by the majority culture (place) within the contextual timeframe (space).

Nonbinary – used by individuals to explain that their gender expression does not fit into the binary categories of woman/female or man/male. Genderqueer is another word used to express the same concept.

Agender – the individual does not identify as any gender.

Genderfluid, gender expansive – words used to self-describe individuals who feel their gender encompasses more than the binary and is more flexible than the binary.

Pronouns – these are the naming words she, he, they etc used to identify a person. These are both culture/language specific as well as individually specific. Using the incorrect pronouns for someone can be hurtful, whereas using a person's correct pronouns can be affirming and supportive. This is particularly important for individuals who are not cisgendered. If you are not sure what someone's pronouns are, it's easy to introduce yourself by name and the pronouns you use, so that they have the opportunity to share their pronouns. E.g. "Hi, I'm Lin, my pronouns are them, they." Some people have their pronouns on their socials and/or their email signatures.

Robyn Ochs is a bisexual activist, professional speaker, and workshop leader who describes the different aspects of gender as on a spectrum from fixed or unchanging to fluid or dynamic. In Robyn's model, sexual attraction can be to people who have gender different to or similar to your own. This is a radical concept that goes beyond the binary.

using scale A:

I experience my gender identity as: ☐
I experience my sexuality as: ☐
I experience my ethnicity as: ☐
I experience my ability/capacity as: ☐

using scale B:

I am attracted to people whose gender identity is: ☐
Most of my friends have an ethnicity that is: ☐
Most of my family have an ability/capacity that is: ☐

Sexual orientation

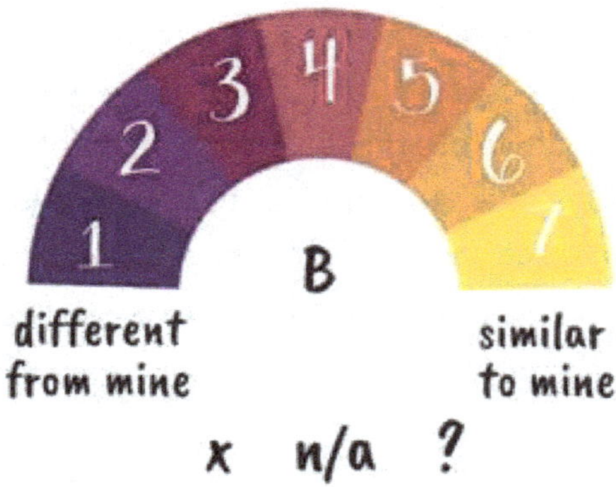

using scale B:

I am attracted to people whose gender identity is:

Sexual orientation or sexuality refers to the way people identify their sexual, emotional and/or romantic attractions. These can differ from the way people express these attractions. For example, you may be a lesbian (a woman who is sexually, emotionally and romantically attracted to women), but you may never have had sex with a woman.

Sexual orientation is not fixed and can be more or less flexible for different people at different points in their lives. This may be because they were unaware that there are other ways to identify or have not had the opportunity to explore and express their authentic selves previously.

Asexual people (aces) experience very little or no sexual attraction to others. This does not mean that asexual people do not want a relationship, some do, and some do not. Some may engage in sexual activities whilst others do not. If you are asexual, it is perfectly fine to be as sexual or not as you are comfortable with. It is important to be open about your asexuality and what that means for you, if you want to have a relationship, so that you can find someone who is supportive and respectful of your sexuality.

Some people describe themselves as graysexual, meaning that have less sexual attraction to others than most people, but not see themselves as asexual.

Allosexual people experience sexual attraction to others. They may be any of:

Heterosexual/straight people are attracted to people of the opposite sex or gender. For example, a cis female who is attracted to men, whether cis or transmen.

(Homosexual) Gay men are men who are attracted to men

(Homosexual) Lesbians are women who are attracted to women.

Bisexual people experience sexual attraction to both sexes. Bisexual+ people experience sexual attraction to all people.

Queer can be used by people to describe being either not cisgendered and/or being not heterosexual/straight. For some people this is an empowering term whilst for others it is associated with trauma and distress.

Demisexual people usually only experience a sexual attraction after they have connected emotionally with someone. Personality is more attractive then looks for demisexual people.

Polysexual/multisexual people are attracted to people of multiple genders, including non-binary and gender diverse people.

Omnisexual people are attracted to people of all genders, including non-binary and gender diverse people.

Pansexual individuals are attracted to people regardless of sex or gender.

Sapiosexuals are attracted to intelligence rather than a particular sex or gender.

Fluid identifying individuals feel that their sexuality shifts and is ever changing rather than being fixed. Some fluid people will use a range of the above terms to describe their sexual orientation in the moment whilst others will say that none of the above terms resonates with them.

6

Sex drive/libido

Your sex drive of libido is the amount which you desire sex or sexual pleasure of any kind. Humans have a natural variation in libido from none to extremely high. Asexual people have no or very low libidos, whilst people with extremely high libidos are described variously as; hypersexual, nymphomaniac or sex addicted. None of these may be true, or they may be. Sex addiction impacts the whole of life in the same way that a drug addiction can.

I have been described as hypersexual and a 'nympho' since I first started being sexual in my mid-teens. In itself, your libido is not an issue. In combination with others, it can be fantastic or problematic. Basically, the ideal scenario is, if monogamous, to be in a relationship with someone of a similar level of sex drive. Both low libido, no problem, both high sex drive, awesome, you are going to have a lot of sex.

However, if you have wildly differing sex drives, this can and does cause a huge amount of friction. Where people are poly or ENM, this can avoid some of the friction as the amount of sex is proportionate to the number of opportunities rather than driven by the partner who has the lowest libido.

It is NEVER ok to pressure or otherwise coerce or force someone into having any kind of sexual intimacy that they do not want to engage in. NO is a complete sentence and does not need to be explained or justified. If you are the person with the higher libido, without external outlets, it can be incredibly frustrating and hurtful.

Mary & Lily - *married lesbian monogamous couple, both she/her*

Mary – we have been together for 12 years but have only had sex twice in the last 5 years. When I hit menopause, I just totally lost interest. That combined with the side effects of my meds for my depression and anxiety, means I just don't even think about sex. Lily used to ask me to talk about my desire or lack of desire and I used to say I would do something about it, like go see my Dr or something, but I never did. I don't worry about her leaving me because we have a really solid relationship.

Lily – I spend my time feeling so undesirable, the lack of sex has really impacted my self-esteem. I used to be some comfortable and confident in my body. Now is Mary compliments me, I cry inside, knowing that she doesn't desire me. I could have sex daily, not having had it for so long is literally killing me. I don't know how to fix it. I can't get my needs met elsewhere as Mary has said we are monogamous and for her, its divorce if I am unfaithful.

Sadly, Mary and Lily's story is repeated in all kinds of relationships all over the world. At some point, for some reason, some people who had average to high sex drives can lose their sex drive. Either that have sex they don't want, to 'keep their partner happy', or they unilaterally declare that their sex life is over.

Having sex you don't want is obvious and even more hurtful to the other person, as well as just being all round a bad idea. So, don't do that. It can be marriage or relationship ending to have a long term 'dead bedroom', unless you BOTH work on some solutions that work for BOTH of you. Also, sex and intimacy can be separate, cuddling and kissing does not have to lead to sex and for some people that can be enough, whilst for others it can destroy the relationship faster.

__Mia__ - Clearly, I have a high sex drive. I would have sex twice a day, every day, if I could. Currently, I run at 4 – 6 sessions a week on a good week and once a week if everyone is busy that week. I have had sexual or play partners who only want sex once a week and I may be their only FWB. I have had FWB who want to fuck as often as possible, and we have been highly compatible. Most of my relationships have been ENM and occasionally poly. This works for me but may not work for someone else. The important thing is to discuss it.

__Paul__ - he/him, straight male, married with a dead bedroom

I love my wife and kids, I really do, but I can't live without sex. Giving myself a hand job is not the same as sex with a willing, interactive human being. I know from all the stuff online I am not alone. I didn't want a divorce, I didn't want to lose my kids or my wife, but I also didn't want to live with this constant sexual frustration eating away at me, turning me into someone I am not.

Now, I don't know if my wife actually meant it, if I am being truly honest. But, during one of my attempts to talk about the last of sex in our marriage, she shouted at me to just go find someone else to fuck if sex meant that much to me. So, I have. I have a really understanding woman who lives way over the other side of town, so we will never run into her when we are in the supermarket or playground. She knows I am never leaving my family, she knows to never ring or text me. We only chat via Telegram, and I am not even sure if she knows me real name, as she never uses my name.

But I can message her when I have some free time and if she's free, she invites me over. We have mind-blowingly good sex and then I have a shower, get dressed and go home. It keeps me sane, and have stopped the massive resentment that I had built up towards my wife for just deciding we weren't going to have sex anymore. I get life happens and the kids are tiring etc, but I truly love her and desire her.

Cheating can end relationships, even when there has been a dead bedroom for years. This is why it is important to actually sit down and work out what can work for you both. What preserves the good things and mitigates the problems. Do not judge yourselves by what the neighbours might think, but by what will work for you both.

Tim *- he/him, straight male, ENM, has one primary partner and other secondaries*

I have a really high sex drive, and my current primary partner does not have anywhere near as much desire for sex as I do. She knows I am ENM and is fine that I have a roster of other women that I fuck when she is not available or in the mood. I would never pressure her to fuck. This way we both get what we want, and it works really well for both of us. I don't know how people can just give up the amount of sex they want for someone else.

If she wanted other to have sex with others, of any gender, I'd be fine with that, just need openness and honesty, and no sex with ex's or friends of ours. That just gets messy.

7

Types of relationships/ connections

The sexual interactions of two or more people, together, for the purposes of sexual pleasure and/or connection are often seen as the core of an intimate relationship between two or more consenting adults. In previous generations in many cultures there were very few options for adult relationships and connections; marriage being the main one.

However, now, in many cultures and contexts there are a myriad of sexual relationships, some that will last for the rest of the people's lives and others that are brief encounters. In other cultures, arranged marriages are still commonplace and dating or spending time alone with the person you are going to marry may be uncommon.

A timeline for relationships used to be something like:

1. Meet someone through a friend or family member
2. Go out a few times (dating)
3. Decide whether or not to be in an exclusive relationship.
4. Start having sex.

Things are a lot more complicated now, particularly in places where online dating or OLD is the norm. Online 'dating' or rather online matching or meeting is not limited to dating apps but extends to websites, virtual reality and social media. Some people have purely online relationships of all kinds, some only have sexual intimacy in real life and some a mix of both. Sex can occur on a first online or in real life meeting, or may never occur or at some stage in and between. Different people have different views on when and how often sexual intimacy is desirable and/or appropriate. As mentioned already, any online intimacy or nudity is out of your control as soon as you hit send. Be very aware that someone you trust today may prove untrust-worthy tomorrow.

8

Dating

Dating can be either exclusive, one person dating or romantically meeting up with one other person, or it can be not exclusive, with one or more of the people involved seeing other people as well. Currently unless an explicit conversation is had to agree to be exclusive, the default position of most people is that spending time with or even having sex with other people is not cheating, because no-one is committed to an exclusive relationship yet.

Ashley *- she/her, straight, ethically non-monogamous (ENM)*

I chatted with a guy online and we really hit it off, the conversation was easy and fun. We decided to meet up, which for me is like a first date or a blind date. But he made it sound like he met up with women all the time and it as nothing special. I let him know I was in an open relationship and saw other people.

I always meet guys for the first time in a public place and make sure my safety person knows when are where I am meeting them and what time they should text or call me to check I am ok. I also tell my safety person where or how I met the guy, so which app etc and also text them any personal details I have of the guy. So, a photo, their name, or at least the name they are using on the app, age, where they live, what job they do etc. I also let first dates know that I have a safety person. If they respond to that with a really stupid response like, 'why do you do that, we live in such a safe area', it lets me know never to see them again. If they are pleased that I have a safety person, it's a green flag.

Anyway, I saw this guy 3 or 4 times over about six weeks, then we started to hang out at my house on the weekends and he's stay over. To me, we were dating, but I am not sure he saw it this way. For him I think I was just a woman he had sex with. He was still talking about other women, and we had not had the exclusive conversation. I figured he knew I saw others because he knew my primary partner's name. Then I broke up with my primary partner.

At this point, I knew I liked this guy, he was smart and funny but would only see me one night a week. My primary is my only boyfriend, the others are FWBs who I play with semi-regularly. So, I asked this guy if he wanted to be my boyfriend. He said yes, but didn't seem to understand what that meant and in hindsight, I should have told him. I did tell him, this meant if he wanted to know what else I was doing with who, as my boyfriend he had the right to know. My previous primary did not want to know. As long as we were both having safe sex all the time, he was fine with it.

This guy never asked any questions, ever, until I said I couldn't see him on the night of the week he preferred to see me, because I was going out with someone else. He was incensed and we had a huge row. I can see now that I should have communicated more clearly. Traditionally dating meant two people meeting up for a 'date', to go somewhere together or do something together, such as having dinner, going to the movies or going to a club. It is not so clear now what a date is or if people are dating. y and be much more up-front with how many FWBs I had and how often I saw them, as he thought when I broke up with my previous primary that meant I was solely seeing him.

Yes, we broke up, no I haven't stopped having sex with him. He has just shifted in FWB as I still like him, he's still good to talk to and he can still make me laugh. I think one person cannot be everything for anyone and ENM or poly relationships are better for everyone involved, as long as no-one gets jealous, and as long as everyone is agreed on how much detail they want about what. I'm always open and honest about being ENM, but not everyone realises what that means.

Dating does not mean that the individuals involved are having sexual intimacy with each other, although they may be. People who do not believe in sex before marriage or who prefer not to have sex outside of a committed relationship are unlikely to have sex whilst dating.

Traditionally dating meant two people meeting up for a 'date', to go somewhere together or do something together, such as having dinner, going to the movies or going to a club. It is not so clear now what a date is or if people are dating.

Online dating refers to people exchanging messages online with the intent to form some kind of relationship with that person/those people. Although for some people there can be mixed messaged with sexually explicit language or pictures being sent prior to consent being obtained, often with a request for pics to be sent back. This is often referred to as sexting and should along with all other kinds of sexual intimacy be safe, sane and consensual.

Some apps and messaging services have functions that time how long an image or text is available before it disappears. However, it is still possible to screen shot on some of these and the override the disappear function on others. In some places, sending unsolicited and unwanted 'dick pics' or other kinds of sexually explicit photos is illegal. It is always illegal if the sender OR receiver are under the age of consent, even if the other party is unaware of the true age of the individual.

There is a perception some apps or services are purely for hookups, though in my experience different people will send exactly the same kind of explicit material through regular text messages as well. If your phone is a work phone, this can be a major breach of your conditions and lead to you losing your job. Having accidentally opened a text message at work from a FWB who had never previously sent or indicated the desire to exchange sexually explicit pics, I know how unexpected this can be.

If you receive sexually explicit content that you want to receive, that is great. If, however, you do not want to receive it, you need to be very clear that it is not ok for them to send this kind of thing to you. Personally explicit photos are not my thing and are more likely to put me off someone that I am not involved with, but I really enjoy consensually sending and receiving sexually explicit texts or emails. It is interesting how few people understand the distinction, with several people sending me links to their favourite porn video rather than sharing a written description of their fantasy.

If you are going to consensually share sexually explicit photos or videos of yourself, you need to make sure that if they are more widely distributed, that you are not identifiable, to minimise any possible repercussions. Obviously if you are an OnlyFans creator or similar, this would not apply as you are wanting to be recognised as that is how you make your money. To decrease the likelihood of being identified, photos and videos should not include your face or any highly identifiable tattoos. Some people use tattoo cover up make up, whilst other use specially designed cover up clothing. You can have your face out of shot or you can use a mask or digital editing to hide your face.

Artificial Intelligence/Bots and porn are synonymous and are quite easily identified by their fake body shapes, sizes and colours as well as their depictions of sexual acts that are almost impossible for real people to do. Porn will be revisited later in this book.

9

Situationships

Situationships exist when two or more people are sexually and/or emotionally involved but not explicitly committed to each other. Sometimes one or more of the people involved are in committed relationships with other people and sometimes everyone involved says that they are single.

Bob *- he/him/thye/them, bisexual, non-monogamous*

So, I basically just love sex, I like to meet people and have fun with them and move on to the next person. Sometimes I just like someone more, so I'll keep playing with them whilst picking up new people on the days/nights that I'm not busy with them.

I'm a commitment-phobe though. I have my own home, car and a good job and I just don't want to lose any of that to anyone through a relationship break up, so anyone long term just ends up in a situationship with me. They either like it or walk away from me.

I don't really do FWBs or fuckbuddies as both of those to me still have a level of commitment. Most of my fun is through hookups but I guess I see a couple of people as more situationships. Both Olly and Jai separately know I am involved with other people, they playfully call me their slut, but I don't belong to anyone. I am here to have a good time.

29

10

Friends with Benefits (FWB)

FWBs are friends who have sex with each other. Sometimes it is an in and between stage between being 'just' friends and being in a relationship, but often it is an open arrangement between friends who are either single or not getting as much sex as they would like in their other relationships. Some FWB arrangements are exclusive, and others are not. These things tend to be more openly discussed than in situationships, where one of the people may be worried they will be dumped if they ask for clarity.

Claire - *she/her, bisexual, polyamorous*

I have quite a few FWBs as I have a really high sex drive and with work and life, it's hard to find time to meet up. A couple of my FWBs are in open marriages, I know this is true as I have verbal consent from their wives to have a FWB with them. Another couple are single dad's so they can only catch up around their kids' schedules, then one is poly so has his primary and I'm one of many others and then a new one is actually single. It suits us all.

I get to have the quantity and quality of sex I like and the variety as I play differently with each one and then get to have regular sex with someone they like who likes them and is understanding of their particular situation.

FWBs for me is just easy going, I text or talk with them in and between when I see them. Depending on how close we are as friends, it could be just a good morning and good night, or it might be an hour chat. I used to have specific days for specific people, but work, mine and theirs, got in the way, so now we just arrange when we want to catch up by text or msg.

David *- he/him, straight, it's complicated*

I was really interested in this woman, she wasn't my usual type, but I just really, really, wanted her. I pursued her for ages, flirting and always popping over to see her after work or on the weekends to hang out. We became really good friends. I'd say I am closer to her than anyone else in my life.

One day I just straight out asked her if we could be friends with benefits because I knew she was lonely, and I was lonely too. She threw me out of her house! But then she called me two weeks later and asked me to come over and talk.

I took condoms on the off chance she had changed her mind, which she had! She said she talked to some of her other friends about it and she couldn't actually think of any good reason to say no, so ok then.

Not exactly a great start but.... We are still friends, but we stopped fucking after 3 years. It had become too much of a relationship for her after a year. I just kept telling her I did not love her and did not want a relationship, but the reality is that after 2 years it was a relationship for both of us. I only ever told her I loved her twice, once when I let her know I wouldn't have sex with her again and once when she was asleep.

My advice would be don't stay overnight, staying overnight shifts the intensity from FWBs to relationship. It seems like a good idea at the time but unless you both want to commit to a relationship, someone is going to get hurt.

11

Fuck Buddies/Booty Calls

Fuck buddies or booty calls are those people you know you can text or call when you are horny, and they are likely to be up for some sex with you. People associate booty calls with 1am drunk texting, but this is not always the case at all.

Evan - he/him, straight, poly/ENM

Sex is my stress release, I really enjoy all kinds of sexual activities. I am mostly into kink, I'm a pleasure dom. I just want to make women orgasm as much as they can. I have my primary relationships, where I have sex, and then I have the women I play with. I do not have sex with them. I play with them, with toys mostly.

When I want to see one of my 'toys', my playthings I just text one and ask her if she is free. If not, I'll move on to the next. I don't really drink, so I am never drunk texting, just wanting my high from playing.

So far, all my playthings are happy to be fuckbuddies, they don't require friendship or a relationship. Mostly they have their own primary relationships anyway and where they don't, they know I do, and this is not on offer.

12

ONS (One Night Stands)/Hookups

ONS are fairly self-explanatory, they are when two or more people meet up and have sex (hookup), not necessarily at night and rarely overnight. Some dating apps have a reputation for being more for hookups or casual sex than for dating. Sometimes this can also be referred to as 'Netflix and chill'.

Fred - he/him, pansexual, single

I am good in bed. I have had a lot of sex, a lot, with a lot of different people. I have ADHD and crave novelty.

For me repeated sex with the same person is really boring even if there is variety within that sex. I much prefer to fuck with different people all the time.

What this means for me is that I pick up new people after work (I work in a bar), or on the apps or online. Men are easier because they will fuck anywhere and don't seem to worry about safety as much, so I can just pick up and we can fuck then and there or see who can host and who has the condoms.

Women tend to want to meet in a public place first, which is really sensible but cuts into the sex time. I like to play for 4-5 hours at a time so this can be hard to navigate as I don't want anyone sleeping over at my place and most women do not want you to know where they live if it is just a hookup.

Anyway, I usually just arrange to meet someone I've met online at a bar near my place and have a quick conversation with; what are your limits, what are you into/not into and what is your safe word. Then I ask if they want to come back to mine to play. Nine times out of ten this works. But then I mainly meet people who already know I have a really high sex drive and want to play for the 4-5 hours, so usually they have a similar sex drive.

The only downside is that some of them want to see me again and it's not personal, it is not that I don't like them, it's just that the first time with someone is what I get off on. For me it is never as good with someone when we fuck again. For most people, it's the opposite of that and the sex gets better the more you learn about the other person's body, what they like and don't. But I have had sex with so many people that I don't want to learn anything anymore! It is possible that I am afraid of commitment, but I still maintain it is just that I prefer novelty.

13

LDR (long distance relationships)

LDR are common and usually occur for one of two reasons; the people in the relationship have an existing in person relationship and one of them has to move for work or study and the other is unable to join them for some time, or the people met online. Where the people met online, and they have not met each other in person or at least video chatted after a few months, it is highly likely that one or more the people are catfishing.

Catfishing refers to setting up a fake online profile to trick people who are looking for relationships. Sometimes people catfish for fun and sometimes to scam people out of money, or to get revenge on someone who has hurt them.

Where LDR are for a short period of time and will revert to or become in person relationships, they can work well. However, when they begin online and are still only online years later, they seem to be far more problematic.

To ensure that you are not being catfished, it is important to videochat with your LDR person/people. Audio chat and texting do not show you that the person is who they claim to be. If you mainly chat via avatars in virtual reality, this applies to you too.

George *- he/him, heteroflexible, monogamous?*

I'm a serious gamer, mainly in VR. I made my last two relationships online in VR. The last one only lasted a few months but was really intense. The one before was much longer. The problem is that I live in another country and no way could we ever meet up. Being monogamous, this meant that neither of us could actually have sex in person with anyone, which kind of defeats the purpose of being in a relationship. VR sex is not the same.

The shorter relationship was with a couple, so we were then a thruple. But they lived together, so I ended up always feeling left out. Would have been different if we could have met in person.

I haven't been catfished yet though, as I always insist on a video chat fairly quickly. Not inappropriately though. One of my friends is online dating and some dude video called her at midnight, whilst drunk....He wasn't catfishing but he was wanting a hookup.

Signs of catfishing:

- The person is telling you they love you, when they have not ever met you or videochatted with you.
- The person telling you they are unable to videochat with you for various reason.
- The person asking for very personal details like your date of birth, address and/or bank account information.
- No online photos or information about the person at all.
- The person asking you for money.
- Their story changing or not making sense.

It is always ok to report and block people who make you feel uneasy or unsafe.

If you are in a LDR, it is important to communicate openly and regularly about how you are both/all feelings and if your needs and wants are being met. If needs and wants are not being met, those difficult conversations should take place.

- What needs to change for this to work?
- Is that change possible?
- Do one/both/all of us want to commit to this change?
- If not, is it time to end the relationship?

14

Committed Relationships

Marriage is not the only form of commitment and people chose to remain together in either an exclusive (monogamous) or non-exclusive relationship for a variety of reasons, not just love or for 'the children'. Commitment is when people chose to have an enduring relationship, which requires work on both sides to ensure the relationship is healthy.

Where only one person is committed to the relationship and the other(s) are not, this person is going to, at best, get hurt and at worst abused. Couples counselling or therapy can help IF both/all parties are committed, but if one person is apathetic or not interested in making the relationship work, nothing can make the relationship work.

Monogamous

Many long term committed monogamous relationships exist where two people of any genders are married to each other or in a civil union together. However, not all marriages are monogamous and not all monogamous relationships are legally registered. In some countries the legal protections offered by marriage are significantly different to those afforded couples outside of marriage. However, for people in a committed relationship with more than one person, marriage is not an option and there is rarely legal protection for all of the involved individuals.

If you are in a two person monogamous committed relationship, it is worth checking out the laws in the country/state/territory/area where you live to look at the options available to you and the legal protections afforded by both.

Mia *- she/her, pansexual*

Recently, I was dating a man who still lives with his ex. They still share groceries and bills and are both named on the lease. The man was shocked to find out that in a few months' time, they will be deemed a defacto couple under the state laws. He said that because they no longer has sex, this was crazy. However, the law would see that they will have been living together for 3 years, sharing financial commitments and day to day practical activities.

It is also always ok to see legal advice prior to any defacto or marriage/civil union to look at how each person can protect the assets that they arrive with. Most relationship break ups are due to arguments around finances, so not being open about these at the outset and discussing financial values and goals can be highly problematic.

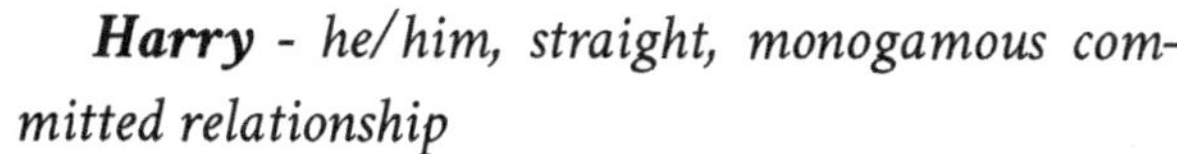

Harry *- he/him, straight, monogamous committed relationship*

I met my partner in high school. We have been together ever since, and we both just turned 50, so that is a long time. We have three kids and the kids used to ask if we were ever going to get married, but it just never seemed necessary. My partner has been a stay at home mum whilst I have worked, but we both wanted that for our kids. Now we have a new business that she works in and when that takes off, I'll be able to quit my main job and we will just work in our little business.

It takes work to parent and stay together, especially if you are not on exactly the same page about how to parent. For us sex is an important part of the relationship and is one of the ways we connect and show our love for each other. I honestly don't know how people can stay together if the sex stops. I know some people as they age, they stop being interested in sex, but not us, I think we both find it life affirming and loving and just fun!

Polyamorous (poly)

Poly relationships involve more than two people. Usually, a poly person will have a primary partner and then other secondary partners, though there are people who live in thruples, where each person has two primary partners. Poly relationships do not work if people become jealous or possessive.

Ivy *- she/her, bisexual, polyamorous*

I'm a single parent and my kid's happiness and wellbeing comes before anything else. This has meant that I have committed to not having a live in partner ever again. I have to say though, that it suits both me and my kid to not to have anyone else living in our space full time.

Over the last ten years or so, I have been exploring my sexuality and a number of factors have come into play, that have led me to where I am today. A secondary partner in a poly relationship and until recently a secondary partner in an open marriage too. I would have described myself as bicurious until I met my now ex-girlfriend. I had been wanting to explore that side of myself for a while but found it really hard navigating the world of online dating and it is so hard to meet people in real life.

I would say that my longer-term boyfriend/partner and I and his primary partner are able to navigate the poly stuff really well. We all have very open and honest communication styles and can all go out clubbing or to an event together, with no issues. However, my now ex-girlfriend, despite having her own primary partner, her husband, really struggled with jealousy. If we were out somewhere together, even if her husband was there too, she would get really possessive of me and jealous if I even talked to anyone else.

Jealousy and possessiveness are totally incompatible with polyamorous relationships. Yes, I might want more time with one of my partners sometimes, but I am not possessive or jealous. I know they and I have enough love to go around. It seems a little odd to me that people think you can and should only ever love one person at a time. I love people that I don't have sex with and I think by saying that only love for one sexual partner and love for a child/parent are valid expressions of love, we diminish the value and place of love in all our lives.

Mia - *she/her, pansexual*

Honest, open communication are required for poly relationships to work well. Polyamory at its best means that someone can have all their different sexual, emotional and intellectual needs met because each partner can meet some of those needs, and together they meet all of the needs. At its worst poly relationships can be a hotbed of anger, frustration, jealousy and regret.

One of the things that I have learnt in my life so far, is that humans have infinite capacity for love if we allow ourselves to. Instead, we often focus on possession and jealously guard 'our' person. I have always believed that if you truly love someone, you want what is best for them. In turn if they truly love you, they do not want things that hurt you.

Sometimes people grow apart and need to break up, but often if we could address and manage the emotions and thoughts behind jealousy and possessiveness things could be worked out. A long time ago I was in a monogamous relationship with a girlfriend. After a year or so, they disclosed that they were really uncomfortable in themselves and wanted to explore the idea of becoming a gay male.

Instead of breaking up straight away or any other number of unsupportive reactions, I suggested we just open up the relationship and they go and try having sex with men who also have sex with men, to see if that really fit. Over a period of time, they experimented and decided that they did not want to transition from AFAB to male, but that we were no longer compatible.

I have no regrets about this at all. I have been in a few monogamous long-term relationships and the rest of my adult life has been ethically non-monogamous. I suspect that I am mostly polyamorous, but currently am ENM.

ENM (ethical non-monogamy)

ENM is where people are non-monogamous, but open and honest about it. Most people in ENM relationships have a myriad of negotiated rules about what is and is not ok to do, share and where they can play with people. ENM people will usually not engage in sexual intimacy with people who are in monogamous relationships as they are trying to be ethical in their behaviour.

Mia - *she/her, pansexual*
I personally don't like to get involved with married people unless their spouse verbally, in person or on the phone or video chat, gives me the ok to do so. Occasionally, this rule has been broken, usually when the married individual has lied. So now, I have a list of questions for people when I meet them online or in person, which end with;

Who do you live with? Surprisingly, people will often tell you then name of who they live with despite having told you five minutes earlier that they are divorced/single. Then it turns out, that they are still in the process of sep-arating....

If you want to know more about ENM there are some excellent resources online and on paper.

Some people engage in ENM so that they can have different types of sex-ual needs met by different sexual partners. At the moment, I have a couple of people I play with in a BDSM sense and then a couple of vanilla people who I just click really well with but with whom ENM works due to busy lives and contextual constraints.

Jai- *she/her, bisexual, ENM*

I just love sex. I love the pleasure of touching, be-ing touched, kissing, everything. My sex drive is so high, that it has been impossible to find one person who can just enjoy in the same quantity that I en-joy. I worked this out as a teenager and have been ENM ever since.

Currently, I don't have any female or gender diverse partners, but that is purely because I am very shy outside of sex, so it is hard for me to meet peo-ple unless it is online. I don't get nervous about first dates or meet ups because I am seeing if I want to have sex with them just as much as they are seeing if they find me attractive. If we don't know offence taken or given, it just is what it is.

Recently I had been trying out this new thing where I don't fuck on the first meet up, but I gave up on that as life is too short to say no, let's wait a few days. I mean, we might not be sexually compatible, so then we probably won't keep having sex. Sometimes I give someone a second try and its nearly always so much better the second time, but if they are someone I can't have a conversation or a good cuddle with then it's a no more from me.

Currently, I don't have a primary. I did for three years or so, but we broke up naturally when things in life changed. Then I briefly did, but I was clearly not thinking right because he was an incredibly lazy lover, who didn't even know I could have multiple orgasms for a few months. I let people know in my online dating profile that I am open to monogamy but am ENM, as you never know!

Open relationships

Some relationships, like mine with one of my early girlfriends, start off monogamous and then for one reason or another, the people within that relationship decide to open it. If both/all people in a committed monogamous relationship are not truly on board with opening the relationship, it will end in a disaster.

Reading Reddit, one would think that nearly all 18-35 year olds are navigating whether or not to open their relationship, usually because one of them wants to 'try a threesome'. I asked one of my recent partners, what they envisaged happening in a threesome. They said very confidently that it would be him, myself (female) and another woman, and the two of us women would be focused solely on his pleasure. I told him he watches too much porn.

Open relationships need rules. Who is allowed to have sex with who else, where, when and how often. Is it ok to have purely sexual interactions, what about if someone 'catches feels' and emptions get involved? Thinking that your partner of any length of time should just let you have a threesome or fuck around because you want to, does not necessarily pass the safe, sane and consensual test or the true love test.

No-one should be getting hurt in an open relationship, which is why the rules are so important and need agreeing PRIOR to any dates or sex with people from outside the relationship. Opening a relationship is very different for different people, there is no one right way to be open, though there are lots of wrong ways. The key to making an open relationship work is respect for your primary partner and open and honest communication. Potential problems need to be identified and addressed before they become issues.

Lola *- they/ them, AFAB pansexual*

I have previously been ENM involved with someone in an open relationship. We each had our own set of rules for our primary partner and then within those rules, negotiated what was an was not acceptable within our ongoing sexual connection. I have also had a really nice initial meet up with a man living with his two female partners who was looking for a cuddle buddy within the framework of his open relationship. He videochatted with one of his partners whilst we were having a drink, to update them on how things were going.

In open relationships, both/ all of the primary relationship individuals are consensually committed to each other, but able to have other sexual and/ or romantic secondary relationships. One of the big pros to an open relationship is the ability for partners with differing levels of libido (sex drive) or differing sexual interests to have their needs met without it damaging the primary relationship.

For example, if one partner has a much higher sex drive than the other, it can enable them both to have sex with other people in ways that meet their needs. I have had ENM play partners who are in open relationships, where their primary partner is the person they are truly committed to, and I am someone they play with to get sexual satisfaction. Meets both our needs and their primary partner does not feel pressured to have sex that they might not want to have.

***Karl** - he/him, straight, exploring an open marriage*

I've been married to my beautiful wife since high school. We truly, deeply love each other. We both have successful careers and have raised 3 kids together. Recently, I noticed that my wife has been unable to get rid of the stress from working so hard. We have a great sex life, good communication and a great marriage in general.

One day my beautiful wife told me that she wanted to video chat with some dude in another continent online. In her underwear. To be honest, this totally threw me. I wondered if I wasn't doing something right or if she wanted to leave me. But honestly, once we sat down and actually really talked through this, and I talked with my life coach (with my wife's knowledge and consent), I could see where she was coming from.

My beautiful wife, wanted to be seen as her, as a woman, not as my wife, not as mum, not as the boss, but as a sexy person. I sat off camera watching her video chat, it really strengthened and deepened our love and trust. I love her so much, I just want her to be happy. She loves me so much, she doesn't want to hurt me.

We have since explored her being able to strip and fuck with another guy, with me there, watching. I was really surprised to find out that lots of couples explore this kind of thing and that it isn't as taboo as I thought it was. We have a new found sexual delight in each other and I am happy for this to be a regular part of our life going forward. We are totally committed to each other, this is just a little fun that we add it now and again!

One common reason people explore an open relationship is the desire to explore their sexuality after many years within a monogamous relationship. Opening a broken relationship will not fix it, it will only bring a heap of new issues to light, such as jealousy or insecurity. However, in a loving, trusting relationship with excellent communication, opening a relationship can strengthen and deepen the love and the relationship.

Swinging/wife-swapping/partner-swapping/the lifestyle

This is where people in relationships consensually engage sexually with others, either directly swapping partners or just having sex with other people within a swinging or lifestyle community. Technically, people who engage in the lifestyle are in an open or non-monogamous relationship, however not all of them will see it like that. For some people the relationship is closed except when attending lifestyle events.

Lifestyle events are usually invite only and an invitation is extended if you know someone who is already in the lifestyle. Single women find it easier to get invites than single men, as most lifestyle events are primarily for couples. Events are usually very clear about the rules around safe sex, though this may not be enforced fully. Many couples involved in swinging feel that this is what keeps their marriage strong, prevents affairs and keeps them honest and open in their communication.

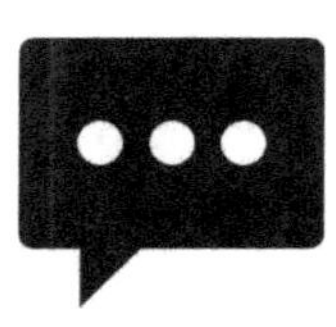

Kaila - *she/her, cis female, non-monogamous*
I met a married man at a swingers' event and his wife was very clear that she is happy for him to keep seeing me as she is too busy and not particularly interested in having sex with him at the moment.

There are a whole host of words for various different ways people engage in the lifestyle such as;

- Unicorn – someone, often a bisexual female, who willingly joins a straight couple for a threesome
- Bull – a male who has sex with the wife/female half of a couple while the husband/man watches
- Cuckold – the husband/man who watches his wife/female partner have sex with another man
- Hotwife – the wife/female partner having sex with another man whilst her husband/male partner watches
- Milf – mother I'd like to fuck – use to describe women over 30 usually

For people for whom this lifestyle works, they get a sexual high from having sex with others and/or watching their partner have sex with others. This is a common theme in porn, but porn is not like real life and without having open conversations first, it is entirely possible that the first time you swing will be the end of your relationship.

Some people want monogamy, others do not. It is important to have these conversations early on, particularly now that no-one is in a relationship until after 'the conversation', no matter how much sex they are having.

15

Stories

This next section of the book is ***part fiction, part erotica***, part educational. The way we learn about sex and intimacy is to read, watch or engage in it. If we don't know what our options are, we don't know what we might want or not want to explore.

Remember, everything you explore needs to be safe, sane and consensual. If you are going to get into the kink world, ensure that you know how to play safely, what your hard (definite no) and soft limits (may be open to exploring but may want to stop at any time) are and how to evaluate if a potential play partner is a safe partner or not.

If you live in an area where there are BDSM classes or meetups, go to those to find out more and start to get a feel for how people interact. Work out who might be willing to share their knowledge and who you might want to avoid.

Remember that vanilla is the best flavour of many things and NOT a term of insult. BDSM or kink are right for some people and vanilla works better for some people, whilst others are happy in either space.

16

Joy

Sexual acts, intimate interactions should be inherently pleasurable, joyful. This is reflected in the use of the word playing to describe sexual interactions with another/others. Playing is often, but not exclusively, the term chosen when the other(s) are not partners, people with whom you are not in any kind of official relationship with.

I was thinking today. I was on a five-hour road trip and had a lot of thinking time. I was reflecting on some Reddit comments about how as few as 18% of women orgasm from penetration alone.

***Anna** - she/her, pansexual, ENM*

One of the last people I played with, asked me if I can cum (orgasm) from PIV (penis in vagina) sex. He was visibly pleased when I said yes. Many women can't and/or prefer to orgasm in other ways. This is perfectly fine, and people should be made to feel comfortable talking about if they want to cum and how they would like this to happen.

I am incredibly lucky, I get so much joy from sex. Pure pleasure. I can cum from my clit as well from penetrative sex and specific sustained touches on specific body parts; nipples being gently caressed, or butt being spanked enough to smart but not so hard it bruises. With a talented play partner, I can orgasm repeatedly until I am lost in pleasure and joy. Usually, this only occurs when I am being submissive (sub) to a dominant (dom) person (of any gender) and is what is called subspace – that headspace where nothing but the pleasure exists.

I was wondering why all these women who don't orgasm from penetration don't as opposed to women like Anna who orgasm easily. Is it a mind thing and is it just that once Anna is turned on, she is, as she told me one person put it so succinctly, '*On On.*' Or is it a skill thing and these women just have lousy partners who aren't interested in their pleasure.

__Anna__ continued: Having had my fair share of these lazy 'lovers' I know that I cum far less if it is all about the other person and not about me at all, but I still cum.

I know a lot of women fake orgasms but I can't be bothered. If I don't find something pleasurable, I will say and ask for something else instead. I hope my partners do the same. They don't all and I was totally shocked by one guy moving my fingers off my clit when he was fucking me, convinced that his penis should be the thing that made me cum.

Maybe we don't just need better sex education about kink, but about pleasure too. That sex can and perhaps should be filled with joy and/or pleasure from start to end. That an orgasm need not be the end, nor even a part if you are having a number of sessions leading to the main session.

Which made me think about why some people like kinky sex as well as, and often more than, vanilla sex. And through discussions with a range of people, I realised it was because in kinky sex, play partners are aiming to have fun and enjoy themselves 99.9% of the time. The other .1% appear to be pretending to be into kink when really they were just seeking cover for abuse. If you meet these people, please report them to the app or online place that you met them, or the police if safe to do so, and then block them everywhere.

Most people enjoy a person who can say "I like (whatever it is they like), how about you?" I respect a person who says "that's not for me but I really like (this), how about you?" I trust a person who doesn't try to get me to do something that I have already said is a hard no, who seeks to communicate openly with both words and body. Nothing is more sexy, than playing with someone who wants to make sure both/all people have as much fun and pleasure as possible, whatever that might look like.

A slow lazy morning quickie (short lasting session of sex), followed by a gentle kiss and cuddle or a full on dom/sub session where control is handed over and used caringly right up to boundaries and 'punishments' are extremely pleasurable…. Both are great if they are what you are into.

When a session isn't going great, relax, take a moment to reconnect to some joy and pleasure that works for the people in that session. Could be a slow kissing chain from head to toe or a spanking that starts gentle and gets firmer and firmer. Could be placing one of their hands somewhere that you are craving being touched. Could just be a cuddle.

These thoughts today made me finally glad that I had sex with some of my 'straight' cis female friends over the years who were 'bored and wanted to try out lesbian sex.' Mostly they just lay there passively and didn't do more than kiss and hug me, which was why I rarely had sex with them a second time. However, I did enjoy seeing their faces light up and their bodies start to move responsively as they slowly realised that they could get turned on from a whole range of touches over different parts of their body that they hadn't thought of as sexual before. That they would finally look at me with eyes that said, 'please touch my clit/pussy now' and only then would I do so, knowing they were 'On On' and ready to just relax and enjoy being brought to orgasm. So beautiful to bring someone else to orgasm, no matter their gender or if they are a hookup, fuck buddy, FWB, play partner or a spouse.

Violet *- she/her, lesbian, ENM*

My first girlfriend spent six months seducing me through great conversation and tickles that finally led to her touching my clit, labia, vulva and vagina. After that we would fuck anywhere and everywhere; the school library, the playing fields, the bus, her living room, the beach. Such joy. And then she went to law school and said she couldn't do these kinds of things anymore.....

Ah well, Vicki thanks for the wonderful introduction to consensual sex, pleasure and joy. You set me up for a lifetime of fun, and helped me to remember that I have the right to enjoy my body with whoever I want (within legal limits obviously), whenever I want. And all those people who judge me can just get lost.

17

Anticipation

Anticipation is such a turn on. Sometimes much more so than an immediate fuck. The negotiations around what you each like and want can be cold and transactional or extremely erotic if you pay attention to the details, anticipating each touch or interaction. Skin on skin, lips and tongue, where they might tease and awaken. Playing over the possibilities, knowing you will get to play soon enough.

Anna's *story continued:*

I love that anticipation, that build up to a pre-planned meeting for sex, or the build up from the moment we both decide that we want to play. The ache deep in my pussy and the wetness that increases as my imagination plays through different ways we can have fun. But there are two scenarios that heighten that anticipation to maximum pre-pleasure pleasure;

1. *The moment I choose to let go and submit and anticipate the rush of pleasure that goes with that. And then*
2. *The moment I know I can dominate as they have relaxed into, or more typically been edged into wanting to submit and give me all the control.*

Both are beautiful and both bring me intense pleasure. I am a switch, someone that enjoys being submissive and being dominant.

Vanilla sex can have as much anticipation as BDSM, it is just talked about less frequently. For me the most pleasurable part in vanilla sex, is the anticipation of skin on skin. To slowly undress the person opposite me whilst I anticipate their reaction to the first time my fingers or lips touch their naked skin. Mmmm And then the pleasure of seeing and feeling their body react to different touches. I love making people wait for me to touch them where they crave it the most, whilst continually building up their pleasure whilst I am anticipating that please fuck me look in their eyes.

Where sex is rushed into, people can miss out on the anticipation, which can form part of the foreplay in both vanilla and kinky sex. Think about all the porn and erotic stories where the Dom (dominant or dominatrix) provide instructions for their submissive on what to wear, where to be and exactly what position to be waiting in. All these play anticipation for both parties to the max. The dom knows what is waiting and can imagine it perfectly, thinking about what they are going to do first. The sub knows they have carried out the instructions perfectly and anticipate their dom's pleasure and therefore their pleasure.

In vanilla sex, the buying of lingerie together can be erotic and set up anticipation beautifully.

18

Good Girl

"Good Girl"

Xena - *she/her, straight*

Just hearing those words from the right person makes my pussy so wet. But when I need to earn those words, it is so erotic, makes me not just wet, but makes my cunt ache.Doesn't really matter whether it's for doing what I'm told or for being attentive and licking and kissing and sucking you until you tell me what a good girl I am.

When your handprints are on my ass, beautiful and red, you carefully caress and kiss them and tell me what a good girl I am. When you let me cum and tell me to be a good girl and cum for you. Cum hard, I do, as often as you let me.

Good girls or good boys or good sluts are individuals who are engaging in a sexually submissive role with a dominant (play) partner. Some people like to live 24/7 in the sub/dom role, whilst others are quite different outside of that sexual play. Most of my friends would describe me as a control freak and very few know that I am a switch and enjoy being submissive just as much as I enjoy being dominant.

Sub/dom play needs to be set up for success. The dom is not 'in charge' as such but both dom and sub create the parameters for the way they will play. For example, if one of the two likes harder impact play (spanking, whipping etc) than the other, it needs to be done at a level that both are comfortable with. Safe words are used to end a play immediately and both dom and sub should have and share their safe word. Safe words need to be words that would never be used accidentally in that context. For example; blueberry is a sensible safe word, dildo is not.

Other people prefer the traffic light system to the use of safe words. The traffic light system in BDSM is a communication tool using red, yellow, and green signals to indicate comfort levels during a scene.

Green means "yes, this is great, keep going," and can also suggest a desire to increase intensity.

Yellow signals a need to slow down, take a breather, or indicates that the current intensity is close to the person's limit.

Red means "stop," indicating that a limit has been reached and the activity should cease immediately. Aftercare should be commenced straight after the activity has stopped.

Discussing what each colour means with your partner before a scene is essential to ensure mutual understanding as different people may have slightly different interpretations. You can either say the colour or touch the colour on a traffic light visual placed within easy reach. This system is particularly useful when trying new activities, allowing adjustments in tempo and intensity without completely stopping.

Being a dom uses up emotion and intellectual energy, whilst being a sub means having trust and being willing to give up control to the dom for the duration of the play. People who live in 24/7 dom/sub relationships may have written contracts and signal their relationship to others through the use of collars or leashes. In public play, a sub should never be approached, one needs to ask the dom if they are willing to share their sub or not. The sub will have already given consent for whatever the dom's answer is. If you do not know who the sub's dom is, it is ok in some situations to ask the sub who they are there with.

19

Need

Julie - she/her, straight, monogamous with non-monogamous partner/fuckbuddy depending on who you ask

I've never felt your need like that before. You just wanted it now. You wanted to fuck hard and take. It was clearly all just about the fucking. But then you held on so tight and cuddled so hard. You don't share your thoughts, so I have no idea what it was all about. If I even figured into it at all. And then, then your weird mood continued. I don't know whether to be angry or sad. I deserve more that's for sure. It costs nothing to say happy birthday. Nothing.

Sure I'm a good fuck. But I'm a person too. With feelings. I know if I say this you will cry. You will say you didn't mean to upset me. So, I won't say anything because this is not about you.

I wonder if you brought your other fuck buddy a present? I've never understood why you choose to spend time with me and money on her. Maybe she has less money than you so you feel more confident with her. You have no idea what I earn, you just know it is a lot more than you. You like to be 'the man' and perhaps I have underestimated the imbalance between us.

I am ready to move on from you. Ready to have value. To share my intimacy with people that appreciate not just that but also appreciate me. As a person. I know there are moments when you do. I know you don't believe I will ever not need you. I don't need you now. You just don't know that.

Sex between two or more people can be emotionally messy, even when it is in theory just fucking and no emotions are meant to be involved. Many people like to fuck for lots of different reasons, including stress release. Whereas, some people only like to have sex with someone they love and/or someone they want a child with. Sometimes, when we don't communicate we can unintentionally hurt others.

Julie continued: The you in this scenario had a complicated relationship with me, we loved each other deeply but refused to acknowledge or discuss it for various dumb reasons. Which meant we sometimes hurt each other. Have I learned from this? Yes and no. Emotions are messy, human interactions are messy, sex is messy. I try and communicate more openly and honestly now.

20

Enough

Rachelle *- she/her, poly*

I am done with fet for now. I am tired of the lies and games people play. Honesty is not hard. Unpleasant sometimes, contact ending sometimes but it is required for true consent to anything. And consent is important in any kind of sexual interaction or relationship. To the very few people I met who were honest. Thanks.

have a love hate relationship with fetlife.com a website and now app for 'fetish life'. It is a worldwide network of people sharing writing, photos and pay for videos, as well as hosting personal ads, networking and meetup groups and message boards. Many of the people on fetlife are honest, wonderful people, but many are dangerous lying individuals out to scam or abuse people by pretending to be into kink. If someone has no friends and follows no-one, they may be new to the site or it may be a red flag and there is no way to know the difference.

A fair amount of people are using fetlife to spruik their OnlyFans or other pay for services whilst many are just enjoying being exhibitionist and sharing themselves or others. There is some non-consensual sharing happening and this needs to be called out and reported when you see it happening. If you are a victim in this, know you are not the first, nor the only and report then block.

Friends introduced me to fetlife and I use it periodically and then don't look at it for months. I have been catfished a few times and had several disastrous meet ups with people from fet. I have also however, met some genuinely nice people, both some I play with and some I don't.

There are groups for all kinds of kinks and fetishes and all locations around the world, both online and in person. It is a good place to browse to see what is out there. Women will rarely respond to messages from non-verified members in online settings, so if you want to connect with women, make sure to be a verified member.

21

Touch

Sometimes it is the smallest touch that turns you on. A gentle caress along a centimetre of your skin, nowhere near your dick. Maybe it is the look that goes with the touch or maybe it's just the chemistry.

Millie - she/her, pansexual

A few of my friends and a few of my sexual play partners over the years have suggested that sex for me is a tactile stim, that I am obsessed with different kinds of touch. There is more than a grain of truth in that. Touch is underrated by people who are quick to fuck and don't engage in much foreplay.

Foreplay is a much needed part of sex that ensures everyone involved is ready for sexual intimacy, which is important to prevent tearing or pain. Touch is the simplest form of foreplay. Touch can be firm or light, a flat palm or a sharp fingernail. It can cover a large amount of the body such as the back or all the way up the insides of legs, or it can be so brief you are not sure you were touched.

Touch can be with your own or someone else's body or with something else like a cat'o'nine-tails or a whip. Touch can be surprising as your or the other person's body responds in expected or unexpected ways. I gently kissed the creases at the edge of someone's eyes and it drove them wild with desire, instant hard on! Most unexpected.

Some people assume that they should be quiet and their body contained during sex, whilst others are happy to vocalise and move their body in ways that make it clear when there are experiencing pleasure. Either way, going straight to genitals when having sex misses out on what can be immensely pleasurable, discovering each other's erogenous zones. An erogenous zone is a part of the body that turns someone on when touched. In a person with a penis, this may result in a hard on and in a person with a vagina, they may get wet. Wetness is not necessarily obvious to the naked eye, so it can also be fun to touch and then explore how wet the person in, explore touch some more and repeat!

Everyone has different erogenous zones, and different types of touch turn different people on. If you have one or more partners, it can show the person/people that you are with that you are interested in their body and that their desire matters to you. For me sex is best is everyone involved in interested in each other's body and their desire demonstrable matters.

22

Context and Levels of Touch

The context of touch involves several key aspects:

- **Intensity**: Refers to how delicate or strong the touch is.
- **Duration**: Relates to how short or prolonged the touch is.
- **Location**: Indicates the area on the body where the touch occurs.
- **Frequency**: Represents the number of touches that happen.
- **Instrument of Touch**: Involves using other body parts, like feet or lips, or objects to create the touch.

Touch can also be categorized into five levels, each serving different purposes:

1. **Healing**: This kind of touch is comforting and often used when someone is sick, tired, or in pain. It can come from a massage therapist, a friend, a nurse, or a partner trained in channelling healing energy.

2. **Affectionate**: Used to show friendship, caring, and nurturance. It includes gestures like a hand on the arm, a pat on the back, or a playful touch, often seen in supportive and encouraging interactions.

3. **Sensual**: Provides sensory pleasure and brings people closer together. Examples include a lingering caress or a shoulder massage

with decadent oil. Sensual touch can be enjoyed for its own sake or lead to more intimate levels.

4. **Erotic**: Associated with foreplay and includes intimate touches like deep kissing or petting that often lead to sexual intercourse. Erotic touch is arousing and full of exciting energy.

5. **Sexual**: Involves any activities that use the bodies for sexual pleasure, such as kissing, petting, oral-genital contact, intercourse, G-spot stimulation, or anal sex. Sexual touch distinguishes itself by focusing on genital pleasure.

23

Honesty

Mandy - *she/her, single, straight*

You say you want a relationship. I check in with you what you really want. You say a friend to fuck. I say thanks for your honesty but, no thanks, I want more than that. Have fun finding that and enjoy. You block me. I say hi, you send a dick pic. I ignore it. You ask for a nude pic. I say no, I don't send them. You block me. You ask if I'm ok with a younger man. I say no problem as long as you are over 30. You say why 30? You get aggressive. I block you.

I am endlessly honest. I'm my profile, in my writing, in my communication. You are not. You being many different people. My pics are me, unfiltered, unedited. My communication is me, unfiltered, spelling and grammar corrected - especially if I typed without my glasses on and then put them on!

I want to matter. Most people want to matter. I find it bizarre that someone feels they matter but the people they are seeking to connect with don't matter. Politeness costs nothing. We cannot all be compatible. I am happy being single, would just rather have a partner. Don't need to be glued to anyone, I like my life. I like alone time and I like those intensely sexual times too. But the people I have sex with matter. I try to be careful of their feelings and I am always honest with them.

I challenge you all to be radically honest with others, about your intentions, your desires and your availability or lack thereof.

So much of sex can be improved with good communication. People lie or aren't open for a myriad of reasons, the main one being fear or rejection or missing out. However, if you are not honest right from the beginning it can snowball out of control quickly. At what point can you come clean and tell the truth without destroying what you have got? Usually, never.

If you are meeting people, either online or in person, be honest and upfront about your situation and what you are looking for. I get more matches when I am ENM than when I am single and looking for a monogamous long-term relationship. However, when I have been looking for a long-term relationship, I have found that with someone else who was looking for that. Not being upfront and honest means you waste your and others time and energy.

We cannot be compatible with everyone, ever. It is better to connect with fewer compatible people than lots of totally incompatible people.

24

Quickie

Ally - she/her, straight, ENM

I love it when you say you want a quickie but I know we have the time to take time. This always brings out the pleasure slut in me and I make sure to touch you in all the ways that drive you crazy with desire whilst showing you how much I am enjoying you.

You give me the control until you just can't stand being teased any more. I know I can restrain you just with one hand until that point, but at that point I don't have the strength to keep you still and nor do I want to.

I want to cum and cum again and again and I know your desire will make sure you fuck me long and hard in ways that make me cum over and over. You love how wet I am and how much wetter I get with each orgasm. You hold on to my shoulders so you can fuck me deeper and harder, your orgasm building slowly and loudly. So much more pleasure than a simple quickie.

Many people in long term relationships find that life gets in the way of finding time to have sex, especially if they have kids. A quickie is one way around that, but even quickies need to be about both/all people's pleasure, not just one person's. Toys such as vibrators, dildos and butt plugs can be really useful additions to ensure that even within a quickie, pleasure is happening for all.

Its ok to hire a babysitter and go out for a few hours on a date or hire a motel/hotel room and have sex in peace. New parents and parents of young children can struggle with feeling 'all touched out' and may respond better to romance and practical support. There is a saying that nothing is more sexy that your husband cleaning the kitchen. This can certainly be the case for parents!

If you are not having sex, or haven't had sex for what seems to you like a while, start the conversation by asking if there are any areas of unmet need in the relationship and not with accusations of not being into you enough. This can be a hard conversation to have, and one that I had repeatedly within a monogamous relationship previously. Which is one reason why I do not envisage that I will be monogamous again.

Relationships where sexual activity has ceased or is minimal are referred to as 'dead bedrooms' and these can occur on a temporary or permanent basis. For some people, this is not a dealbreaker and for others it is. I do not regret staying in my previous relationship, but I would not do it again. Stress kills many people's sex drives, but for some people, sex is a great stress release so the more stressed they are the more they want sex.

Mental health difficulties and hours worked/studying can also impact sex drives, usually negatively. Being a new mum means that sex should not happen for around 6 weeks, but longer if the birth trauma to her body is significant. Many partners do know understand this and can feel slighted or unwanted, when in reality the new mum's body needs time to heal first.

Not having privacy can also impact on people's willingness to have sex. Some people are happy to risk having semi-public sex in a car or park after dark, whilst others are not. Neither is right or wrong, though technically public sex is illegal in most parts of the world. With the cost of living crisis currently gripping much of the world, more and more adults are having to move back in with older parents when they experience a relationship break up. This can significantly impact how often they are comfortable having sex.

Personally, I am not very comfortable having sex with someone in my or their parental home, if someone else is home. However, I am totally fine with having sex in a tent in a campsite!

The lack of personal space has led to even more loneliness and disconnection in a range of adults, those who have never left home and those who have bounced back due to life circumstances. It can be very tempting to have a quickie with anyone who offers it if you are feeling lonely and/or have no personal space. If people ask if you can host, it means can we go to your place for sex. If you love with others, but are comfortable bringing someone back for sex, it is better to be clear about who you live with. If you just say yes, the implication is that you live by yourself.

Quickies can be very pleasurable and extremely sexy if they feel like snatched moments of fun. They can also be disappointing and not much fun if they are as a result of premature ejaculation or interruption by the kids. Premature ejaculation or any ejaculation does not need to be where sex ends, it can be at the start, in the middle or at the end. If you cum and the person you are with has not but wants to, ask them what you can do to help them cum, or what they would like to do to cum.

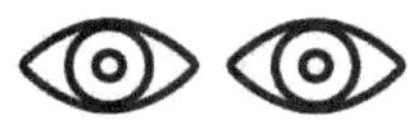

Anna - she/they, bisexual, non-monogamous
One of the people I play with likes to watch me play with my clit and pussy until I cum. This often turns him on so much that he wants to fuck and cum again. Another person doesn't like me to play with myself but will happily lick my clit and either finger me or use a vibrator on me until I cum.

The people who lose interest once they have cum but I am not yet satisfied are not people that last in my life. And that's ok, like I keep saying we can't all be compatible all of the time.

25

Trust

Any kind of sex is better with trust. But without trust, any kind of kinky sex is a no from me. Very interesting how some 'Master's' can claim to be a true Master and then operate under wholesale deception. Wonder how many women in the kink community experience this and how it impacts them going forward. Wonder how many men suspect one of their friends or acquaintances are doing this and don't stop it.

Safety is more than just physical safety.

A Master or a Mistress is a top or dominant/dom/domme in a BDSM situation. Kinky sex may or may not involve a dom/sub dynamic but where it does, it is vital that there is trust. Never ever let someone tie up or otherwise restrain you so that you cannot leave UNLESS you know and trust them AND they are in control of their actions. Restraints also need to be safe, they should not restrict blood flow at all.

Elle - she/her, submissive

The last person I played with that took poppers lost control of his actions, refused to take no for an answer and I ended up non-consensually bruised up. I refuse to play with anyone who is on any drugs or has had more than one alcoholic drink now. I lose a lot of potential play this way, but I am keeping myself safe. It is incredibly scary to be alone with a much larger more powerful person who will not take no for an answer AND thinks you are still consenting to be their submissive.

Questions that should be asked of potential BDSM play partners:

- How long have you been into BDSM?
- What are your experiences?
- What are you looking for?
- What are your hard limits?
- What are your soft limits?
- Is there anything you are particularly interested in exploring?
- Have you got a clean sexual health check recently?
- Do you have any physical limitations or restrictions that I need to know?
- What kind of aftercare do you need? Aftercare refers to the interactions after the sexual play has stopped but before you go your separate ways and often involves some cuddling.

You can also ask specific questions around particular activities:

- When was the last time you were tied up/restrained or tied up/restrained someone else?
- What kind of restraints work best for you and why?
- Do you like obedience or some battiness?
- Are you open to anal toys and/or anal sex?
- How long are you comfortable having sex for?
- What is your longest play session?
- How do you want to be addressed/what should I call you? (subs ask this)
- Are there any names that you cannot be called? Are there some that particularly turn you on? (doms ask this)

- What is your favourite fantasy? Is this something you want to happen in real life or should it stay a fantasy?
- How hard do you like impact play? Leave your skin pink/red? Leave bruises? Leave welts?
- If you get into subspace what do you need to keep you safe/come back into yourself? (dom asks this)
- What supports you to feel/be dominant?
- What kind of sub/dom would you describe yourself as?
- How have others described you?
- Do you enjoy edging or orgasm denial/control?
- Would you prefer to beg to cum or beg not to be allowed to cum?
- Do you want to punish/be punished for transgressions?
- How do you want to punish/be punished?

Bear in mind that because each person interacts with another differently, the answers to these questions are rarely static for all people.

Yasmin - she/her, submmissive

I do not allow myself to be in subspace with many people. The ones I do, I trust implicitly. This was not always the case.

As a young woman I had what I now know was an extremely abusive relationship with a woman who pretended to be into BDSM, but really she was just abusive. Consent was not a part of her vocabulary and because I did not know any better and because it was a toxic relationship, my self esteem had plummeted. I believed her when she said that she did these things because she loved me, or because I deserved them.

This experience has shaped how I dominate when I am dominate. I refuse to physically hurt someone. I can leave a hand print that fades rapidly but I cannot bruise or mark someone's body. I cannot degrade them. I prefer to verbally restrain and my aftercare is compulsory. It takes a lot for me to trust someone enough to give them the gift of my subspace. It should take a lot of trust for any sub to give this gift.

26

Pleasure

Nina - *she/her, straight*

I tell you that when we meet you need to dress smart casual, and to arrive early or on time. Anything else shows you do not really want to be submissive.

You dress carefully, wanting to get it right. You message me a photo of you just before you leave home as instructed. Slightly nervous, you wait for my reply. 'Acceptable and sexy' is the three word text you get in response.

Slightly early at the assigned meeting place I watch you arrive. Dressed exactly as described on the outside, I wonder what you are wearing underneath. I greet you with a 'hi, wait and see. I'm hungry, let's eat first.'

Over dinner I tell you how much I am looking forward to playing with, teasing and turning you on by touching, kissing, sucking, pinching and nibbling your nipples. How when they are hard as possible I will take them into my mouth one at a time and suck and lick and kiss and bite them until you are ready to submit because you are craving pleasure from other parts of your body too.

As I am talking quietly, my composure is maintained but you are starting to get hornier and hornier and it is showing in your breathing, hard on and the look in your eyes.

I gently touch your arm, asking if you want to play yet. You nod and I quietly but firmly tell you to give me a full answer. 'Yes please, I want to play

83

now.' You respond beautifully and I reward you with a kiss on your lips. A slow gentle kiss that pulls at your lips and conveys desire.

Time to see the other sexy underwear I tell you whilst standing up and holding out my hand. You take my hand and I lead you back to where we are going to play. I open the door and tell you to wait for a few minutes. I will open the door when I am ready for you.

When I open the door all that I have on is a black lacy very short dress. I tell you to come in and stand very still so that I can undress you slowly and discover every part of your body and which kind of touch you prefer. It is so hard to stand still when I keep going back to tease your nipples in and between unbuttoning your shirt and pants.

Every inch of your back and chest is kissed, caressed and touched. But each time you move into or away from a touch I remind you that you are meant to be standing still for me and that until you can, you cannot touch me at all. I will not let you lick my pussy and pleasure me until you do as you are told properly. Even so, I let you lay down so that it is easier for you to be still. Once your cock is hard and your body still, with one hand I caress a nipple and with the other I trace up and down your cock.

Well done, you can lick me now.
Once you start though, I tell you that you cannot stop until I cum at least twice, that you need to earn my touch on your cock again, that you cannot fuck me until I have had my fill of your tongue on and in my pussy, pleasuring me.

No matter how you set up your play/intimacy with known or new people, you need to ensure you have the framework laid down for the time to be safe, sane and consensual.

27

Wanting

*A**lex** - she/her, bi, Dominatrix*
You say you want. You want to serve. You want to adore. I wonder if you know what these mean. I ask you to define your parameters of time, place, and limits. You say you have no limits, but when I provide mine you share a few. You tell me you want to serve me at all times and I say no. I only play outside of work. To which you seem surprised but are unable to provide me with any actual real availability.

I tell you that I am not interested in dominating through fear. I like to dominate through desire. To build that trust where you can fully submit in honesty and truth that submission is your desire. You say you adore this. But I know you are not ready to own your truth. And that's ok. I have given you an easy out even though this was all of your instigation and not mine.

I own my truth. I like to submit at times, truly submit to offer my body to my lover, my Dom/Domme, to give them the choices and control. In my truth I can beg to cum and I can thank them for a punishment. Both are equally pleasurable in this state. I own my dominant truth too. I am a kind domme mostly. I seek to discover your desire and heighten it. You are scared of this, which is fine.

I do not need to do this, but with the right person it is so pleasurable. I love to see that ache In someone's eyes as they let go of the control and slide into desire. I love to feel a body arch up to meet my touch when I have told the person to be still. The look in their eyes when I move my hand or lips away and say calmly and quietly, 'I told you to stay still.' I love how some people will deliberately move to seek a punishment and then be frustrated that what they wanted was not forthcoming, until they realise I knew exactly how to punish them in ways that met their truth of how they secretly desire to submit.

I do not need to domme or sub, I can just be. I can just enjoy sensual play and gentle play. My truth is I love touch, I love physical interactions within my boundaries of no lasting pain, no bruising, no cutting. Each type of touch is so pleasurable, to give, to receive.

It's ok that you are not ready. I am not going to spend time and energy persuading you. When you are ready, come back and ask again. But, you will need to prove you are ready. Saying you want and actually wanting are two very different things. When you actually want, you probably won't need to say anything. The way you look and move will say it all.

I could give you all the parameters I am asking you for, but I am trying to teach you something that you are not learning. Setting up a D/S relationship of any kind is all about the setting up. And that is consensual and caring. It is not about throwing yourself at someone and saying I am yours. Do what you will. Because that will is dependent on what desires can create the greatest desire for both people.

It is not all about blatant power dynamics. It is about carefully considered words and touches and toys that give you that freedom to let go and be the slut you so clearly want to be. But you are afraid to be. Done wrong D/S play can totally mess with your head. When you understand what aftercare means and can tell me what aftercare works for you, then I can truly contemplate being your Mistress.

I like to take care of my belongings. I do not use them and throw them away. I like to nurture and grow a relationship, no matter what kind it is. You say you ache to be my little slut, but you are not ready. Perhaps I will want you when you are ready and perhaps I won't. If I don't, the work you have done will not be in vain. I worry for you, you are so vulnerable in your not fully thought through desires. You think that vulnerability is part of be-

ing in this kind of relationship. It is not. It is a totally different vulnerability that sits at the heart of any relationship I have as a Mistress.

That vulnerability is two fold; openness and honesty, with yourself and with me. In turn, I let you be who you desire and I bring you on a journey of discovery, with care. And discipline, and power, and domination. But without the openness and honesty, I am not interested.

Alex explained to me that one day she had found a message in her fetlife inbox, from a guy who has recently moved to the city she lives in. He had read her profile and some of her writing and seen her photos. He wrote to ask if he could be Alex's submissive. He wanted to be totally controlled in two spheres; financially and sexually. Alex told me that she has not ever been and never will be a financial dominatrix, it does not interest her in the least.

Within financial domination, the submissive hands over a chunk or (or all of) their pay and the dom/domme pays their bills for them and may or may not buy them gifts etc but may also spend the money on themselves.

In response to this he offered to pay Alex, which she equally was not interested in, despite knowing the money would be useful. Then this guy offered to clean Alex's house and do her gardening for her, if she would dominate and degrade him. Alex shared how she was sorely tempted at this as she hates cleaning and is a very lacklustre gardener. He claimed to have had a Mistress in his previous city and sent Alex a copy of the contract he had signed with her. Alex shared that they video chatted a little, but that she was continually frustrated with his lack of openness.

It turned out he was married with kids and in fact hid this side of himself from his wife. He could not name any limits when Alex asked and despite not actually being available 24/7 due to his work and his wife and kids, he spent a few weeks fixating on being there 24/7 to serve Alex. Alex remains puzzled by how his wife didn't know that he had been giving his previous Mistress half of his salary for several years and cannot imagine how devastated his wife will be if she ever finds out.

To not name your limits in any kind of relationship is frankly stupid. Everyone has a limit, whether it accords with the law or not. In Alex's case above, the man wanted to send her videos where he was submitting to Alex to demonstrate his seriousness, but could not agree an actual date, time or place to meet when Alex put forward that they needed to meet in person.

Alex continued:

I was willing to meet because sometimes people are more open in person than online. I have a healthy skepticism of people online and assume they are not being 100% honest, even though I am. And I know it can be hard to text that you are or are not into water sports (urine play) or scat (poo play). One of the people I play with says that when people say they have no limits, he asks them if he can shit in their mouth then! He is not into this at all, but just likes to push people's buttons to show how stupid saying you have no limits is.

I won't domme or sub with anyone that says they have no limits because it can be dangerous. No limits means that skin can be bruised or cut, bodily fluids or waste put in or on the body, objects used in or on the body without limit. Everyone should have limits. If they don't, they are not ready to play in a safe, sane and consensual way. My limits may vary slightly with different people, but my hard limits are always a NO. One of my flexible limits is around restraint. I attended BDSM rope workshops years ago and these always started with discussions around safety in BDSM.

28

Restraints/bondage

RJ - *she/her, submissive, bicurious*

I will not let someone inexperienced tie me up or use any form of mechanical restraint on me (such as handcuffs, spreader bar etc). Nor will I let someone I do not trust do so. However, someone experienced who I trust and am submissive to is more than welcome to restrain my hands/arms and feet/legs.

A regular FWB spent almost 6 months building trust with me before I let him restrain me, whereas another was allowed on our first play. It is really important to err on the side of caution and trust your gut. If in doubt, do not get tied up! I won't be a rope bunny (tied up) for this as it often involves immobilisation of the body in ways that I personally am not physically comfortable with. I prefer wide leather cuffs, lined with a soft fabric and cushioning. Personal preference.

If you want to get into this scene learn both how to restrain AND experience being restrained, so that you can understand some of the physical sensations that restraint can bring about. The erotic/sexual sensations are highly individual too. Sometimes I can just see the spreader bar, which fits between my ankles to keep my legs spread apart, and get incredibly turned on. Other times, I might occasionally say not today. To be fair, I have done that once, but humans are emotional creatures and we are rarely totally predictable.

Someone who is physically restrained should never be left alone, in case they experience a medical emergency or issue. Some of the positions commonly used in bondage can restrict blood flow, leading to tissue damage if they are not corrected. Shibari is a form of rope play that looks beautiful when done.

Regular precautions when engaging in bondage are never leaving the restrained person alone, never playing under the influence of alcohol or drugs and always having scissors or a knife available to cut the rope in case there is an emergency.

Issues that arise most frequently are due to the blood flow being restricted. Issues arise gradually and permanent damage can be avoided if the person is released from their bonds. Symptoms of blood flow restriction are temperature drop of the area, numbness, and colour change. Where the skin becomes red, then purple the blood is able to flow properly in vein. This can be prevented by ensuring the restraint is loose enough for two fingers to be placed under the rope/cuffs, which is NOT suitable for suspension play. Blood flow restrictions are particularly dangerous around the head and around the penis and balls.

If the blood flow through an artery is restricted this is more dangerous and can be identified by the arm/leg going white. Nerve damage is the most serious issue and can cause permanent damage. This can happen very quickly and can be irreversible, with indications being pain, numbness or loss of feeling.. This is why people who want to engage in bondage should take classes so they can learn where the body's nerves and how to restrain without impinging on the nerves.

Rope

Rope play or rope bondage uses ropes to restraint/restrict movement, or wrap, or suspend a person, as part of BDSM play. Rope play does not necessarily lead to sex and may be the whole point of the play.

Shibari and kinbaku originate in Japan and are highly stylised. This is the kind of rope play often depicted in porn or the media. It requires a high level of skill and can take a significant amount of time.

In all rope play it is important to use ropes that will not chafe or burn the skin and are easy to manipulate. Ropes need to be strong enough that they will not break, particularly if being used for suspension. However, they need to be able to be removed immediately in case of a medical emergency or use of the safe word.

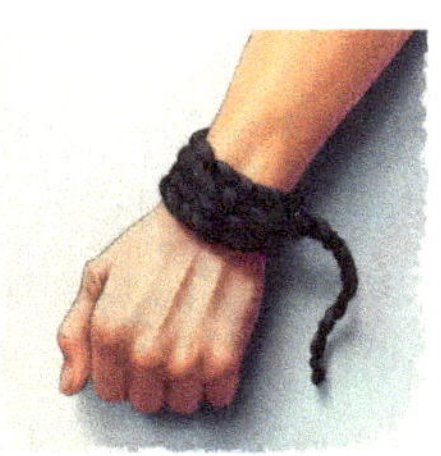

Suspension play can result in dizziness or nausea which can lead to fainting. A person should be untied immediately, put into recovery position and kept warm. Play should be stopped for the day. Once the person feels better, the people involved need to discuss what went wrong to find out why and evaluate the safety of playing in this way again. In suspension play a person can be fully suspended, or partially suspended. Safety is paramount in suspension play, with some people having a third person there who is solely there for safety.

Handcuffs/ankle cuffs

Metal handcuffs are the least comfortable and most unsafe types of handcuffs to use. Cuffs are often used as tie points for chain or rope, but can also be used to restrain the hands or ankles together. Cuffs need to be able to be removed easily in case of a medical event, so ones that use keys should never be used in case the key is lost. If cuffs are going to be bearing any weight, such as when being used with a X-cross or standing frame, they need to be used in ways that will not cause nerve damage. This is one of the reasons that buckle-up soft lined leather cuffs are popular.

Spreader bar

Spreader bars are designed to be put between the ankles of someone who has their legs spread, in a sitting, standing or lying position. The spreader will usually have cuffs on either side and can also be used to restrain hands in a sitting or lying position. Spreader bars can be bought or made. Ensure there are no sharp bits that can cause injury if making yourself.

Collar

Collars are usually used within a BDSM relationship to signify that the collar wearer is owned by someone. That someone may be holding a leash which is attached to the collar or they may not. Collars that have a solid metal ring are able to be used for restraints by attaching a chain/leash/rope to the collar and then to another point, or the same point having looped around or over the body, often over the genitals.

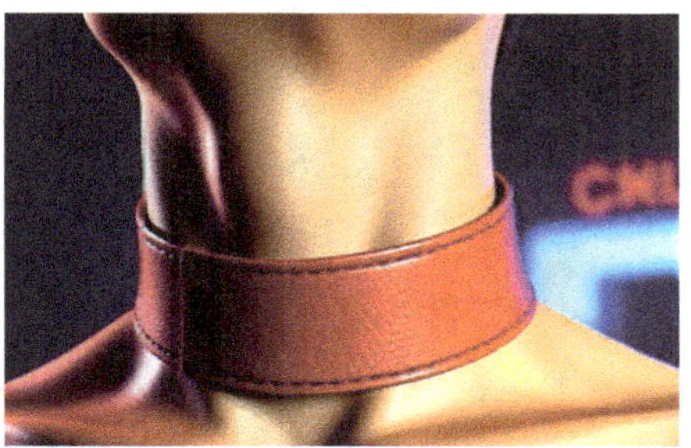

Gag

Gags should never be used with individuals who have breathing problems such as asthma, or who have a cold etc. Gags go into the mouth to prevent someone from talking or making a sound. The may be held in place by a strap around the face or the person may have just be told to keep the gag in place. Care should be taken that the person is always able to breathe when a gag is being used. Mouth and nose should NEVER both be covered.

Full face mask/bondage hood/gimp mask

A full face mask/bondage hood/gimp mask is a hood that can be used in BDSM play for head bondage, restraint, sensory deprivation, objectification and/or depersonalisation. They are usually made from rubber, latex, PVC, spandex or leather with holes for each nostril. Some have holes over the mouth and some do not. As with gags, these should never be used with people who have breathing issues, and the mouth and nose should NEVER both be covered.

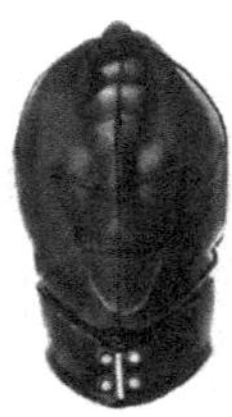

Full bondage suit/gimp suit

Made from rubber, latex, PVC, spandex or leather these full body suits may have a range of openings for 'easy access'. They may be used for bondage/restraint or because people just like the look of them. As with hoods, these should never be used with people who have breathing issues, and the mouth and nose should NEVER both be covered.

Verbal restraints

Verbal restraints are spoken commands given instead of using actual, physical or mechanical restraints. For example, stay still or don't move. These can be used in play where people are very much BDSM or mostly vanilla. It is the set up of how they are used and the consequences for not following the commands that determine whether it is a more BDSM or vanilla play.

29

Power differential relationships

Some people really like power differential relationships to be followed 24/7, such as 'trad wives' and their husbands and kids, who follow a 1940s and 1950s American suburban family 'ideal' where the husband works and the wife takes care of the home and children and is often sexually subservient to the husband. The submissive who contacted Alex in a previous chapter, would have been available to serve her for a few hours a week.

Nearly all 24/7 power differential relationships involve a signed contract that sets the terms and conditions of the relationship and names the relationship and the people within it. Many power differential relationships are not 24/7 even if the only two (or more) people involved live together in a committed relationship.

Alex continued: *About 6 months ago, I had a second submissive contact me through fetlife. This person wanted to be my live in slave. They wanted to pay me rent to sleep on the floor at the bottom of my bed, or in the bathroom, and to do all my cleaning, gardening, household chores etc. In return they wanted to be degraded verbally and kept sexually frustrated through the use of a 'cock cage'. Tempt-*

ing though it was to have all my housework done for me, I have an inability to verbally degrade someone for more than a few seconds in the heat of an argument.

I have no judgement against those that wish to enter into these kinds of relationships as long as everyone sets everything up consensually at the beginning. Consent needs to be informed, exactly what is being agreed to, for how long and in what context. For example, if we are in role in a public place and a work colleague comes to talk, is it ok or not to break role.

All of the following types of power differential relationships can take place in real life or online only or a mixture. Some will have no sexual contact and others will involve one person fully submitting to the other as their 'fuck toy' to use as they would like.

In some of these relationships, the submissive may be shared with others, whilst in others they will not. Again this should be negotiated at the start of a relationship, or as it evolves and changes as necessary. Some people do not use any of these labels or indeed any labels, whilst for other people the label is of great importance.

Dom/Sub or Domme/Sub (D/s)

In D/s, both people get sexual or erotic pleasure from either dominating or being dominated. Those who dominate are called Doms (regardless of gender) or Dommes (female), while those who are submissive to the Dom are called submissives or subs. Sometimes a Domme may be called Dominatrix.

D/s may be a relationship style or a kink that is enjoyed anywhere from rarely to 24/7. Where someone enjoys both dominating and being dominated, this is referred to as being a switch. I am, and have always been a switch. I very much enjoy both roles within very clear parameters, that do not involve hard core pain at all.

D/s play and/or relationships should always be defined by the people within them, not the people outside of them. The parameters of who does what, when and why are between and matter to ONLY the people in the relationship/play session. Just because a particular act, for example wearing no underwear, may be seen as submissive generally, it does not mean that all subs must do that and no Doms would.

Safety is paramount in D/s and should be renegotiated as often as needed. Aftercare should be explicitly discussed and incorporated into D/s play/sex.

Master/Slave or Mistress/Slave

Sexual slavery in a BDSM context is both a sexual fantasy and sexual roleplay. Again as with D/s it can be anything from every now and then sex/play session to a 24/7 lifestyle. Some people find the language around slave very confronting and/or offensive, whilst for others it is the only word that describes ownership of another person in the way they want to present the concept.

Where Master or Mistress and slave relationships are set up to be ongoing or at least long term, they are often following rules contained in a signed contract. This contract is designed to explain the rules and parameters of that relationship. Some Masters and Mistresses have more than one slave. Some live with their slaves and others do not.

If you want to learn more about these kids of relationships the 2014 book by Raven Kaldera, Paradigms of Power, Styles of Master/ Slave Relationships is an excellent resource.

Daddy/little/baby (girl or boy) DDlg or Mommy/ little/baby (girl or boy)

This is a form of role play or kink that involves consenting adults ONLY. The 'little' role plays age regression and may or may not be submissive to their 'caregiver' in the relationship. This is another type of power exchange relationship that can be live in 24/7, part time or occasional. Where it is ongoing, the people involved may choose to have a contract.

It is important that the contract does not hide or cover financial or other abuse. If you are exploring being a little or baby, it is sensible to meet others in the lifestyle and talk through options before jumping into a 24/7 contract.

Human pets

Human pets refer to role-playing or consensual power dynamic relationships or play within the BDSM or kink communities. Human pets, adopt behaviours and characteristics associated with a particular animal, while another person play the role of their owner or handler.

The concept involves elements of control or domination and submission, where the pet may engage in submissive behaviours like obeying commands, wearing symbolic accessories like collars or leashes, and sometimes moving or communicating in animal-like ways. The owner or handler typically takes on a caretaker or dominant role, providing guidance, structure, and sometimes discipline within agreed-upon boundaries.

Again, this dynamic needs to be agreed on in safe, sane and consensual ways based on mutual trust and respect. Both parties actively negotiate and agree upon the roles, behaviours, and limits involved. Consent is fundamental and must be freely given, with clear communication about boundaries and expectations.

While the roles may mimic aspects of pet ownership, legally and fundamentally, humans are not considered pets in the same sense as animals. The dynamic is primarily symbolic and psychological. This kind of role-playing can lead to deep intimacy, exploration of power dynamics, and mutual pleasure.

Participants in human pet play emphasize the importance of safety, respect, and understanding of each other's desires and limits. It's a unique form of expression and connection that can vary widely in its practices and meanings from one couple or group to another, always guided by the principles of mutual consent and enjoyment.

Zig - they/them, pansexual

I met someone online, and then we met up in person. I was interested in exploring being a human pet. They were happy to have a couple of sessions with me at their home where we engaged in some pet play. In these sessions, I was their cat in the first session. They had me move around on command and lick water from a bowl on the floor command. They would caress me and encourage me to curl up around their feet.

The second session, we switched it up and I role played their horse. In this role play, I was a horse in need of training. This session was quite different to the first session. We had talked about some of the variety of experiences that pet play encompasses and my 'owner' was happy to share a few of these with me as an introduction. We did chat for a few months first to agree what my limits were and what they were willing to do.

I used my safe word during the horse role play as I discovered that I really am not into having a riding crop used on my butt! My owner stopped straight away and held me and stroked my hair like they had when I was their cat. This was our agreed aftercare and it really helped make me feel safe and centred again.

I will definitely seek out this kind of play in the future, as a cat. But, its not something that I personally want to do 24/7, like someone I met at a kink meetup. But I guess that is the joy of kink play, everyone can just be themselves.

30

Sissy

In kink or BDSM communities, the term "sissy" typically refers to a person who embraces or explores aspects of femininity that are traditionally associated with women. This exploration often involves a deliberate and exaggerated performance of femininity by someone who may identify as male or who may have a masculine gender expression.

The concept of being a "sissy" is often bound up with themes of gender play, submission, and humiliation within a consensual and role-playing framework. Individuals who identify as sissies might engage in activities such as dressing in traditionally feminine attire (such as lingerie or dresses), adopting feminine behaviours and mannerisms, or participating in scenarios where they are encouraged to act in a submissive or subservient manner.

For some individuals, exploring sissy play can be a way to explore and express aspects of gender identity, role-play fantasies, or power dynamics. It's important to note that participation in sissy play is consensual and typically involves clear negotiation of boundaries, desires, and limits between all parties involved.

Ultimately, sissy play is a form of sexual or erotic expression that can vary widely in its practices and meanings from person to person or from one relationship to another. Like other forms of BDSM or kink activities, it requires mutual respect, understanding, and communication to ensure that all participants feel safe, valued, and fulfilled in their exploration. Safe words and aftercare need to be agreed on and used as needed.

31

Slut

Slut can mean so many different things to different people in different contexts. It can be used as an insult, a word to humiliate. It can be reclaimed as a powerful statement from someone who loves sex. It can be used by a dom/domme with their submissive affectionately, possessively, factually.

Is a slut someone who has lots of sex with lots of different people? Is a slut someone who enjoys the sex they do have with one or more people with openness and joy? Is a slut someone who just has or is perceived to have more sex than the person calling her a slut?

Why is slut associated with women more? What do we call males who love sex or who have a lot of sex? Stud... Feel the difference in the word.

Mia - *she/her, pansexual, ENM*

I love sex, I love having a wet cunt. I love edging and being denied orgasm until I can no longer hold off. If this makes me a slut, then for me slut must be a good word.

I love exploring a partner's body and playing with their desires. Is this a good thing? Bad thing? Who knows? For me this is just a factual statement.

Do I want to fuck everyone I meet? NO. I only want sex with people I like, with people I have some form of connection with, with people who are open and honest. But when I want it, I really really want it.

Sex is divisive, many of my friends are happy never to have sex, others are like, 'if I have to, then its once a week to keep my partner happy.'
I on the other hand am happy to have sex at any time of day with a partner I like and am comfortable with. I want to give them lots of pleasure, not just by sharing mine but by working out what drives them wild and then doing it. Even when they assume that a blowjob (if male) is what will give them the most pleasure possible.

Blowjobs are not my thing... but gently kissing all around the base of a cock, stroking and moving my fingers over their cock, balls and groin until they are aching with desire.

Nipples are so beautiful on anyone. So nice in my mouth or between my fingers. I guess I aim to release the inner slut in the person I play with... To free them to enjoy with abandon. To be open to pure pleasure.

People deserve to know the joy that can be experienced with amazing sex with a person they are connected with. Not the shy awkward sex of a first date or the bad sex where they don't care about your pleasure, nor you theirs. But the whole body and mind involved, full on drive to give and receive as much and as intense pleasure as possible.

Anna - *she/her, straight*
There are a couple of people over the years who have got to see my 'inner slut' in all her full glory. People who delight in my pleasure as well as theirs. Most people I have sex with never see this side of me. I will only share this with someone I know will enjoy it and not judge me negatively.

In many cultures, cis women used to be think that they could be either a 'whore or a virgin', meaning that a cis woman who wants to be in a long term committed relationship was given the impression growing up that sex was not a pleasurable act, it was one of duty. Women who openly enjoyed sex were put down and mocked. It was only in the 1960s that this messaging started to change.

Sara - *she/her, bisexual*
The people that do that show me they enjoy my enjoyment are the ones that get to see my inner slut. One of them would even ask me, "Is your inner slut ready to play yet?" He loved seeing me in that state of pleasure and raw sexuality.

In contrast, I have fucked with people that have no idea that I am multi-orgasmic, let alone know exactly how much I can and do enjoy sex with a compatible sexual partner or partners. I have met men, women and non-binary people who hide the potential extent of their pleasure my minimising the amount they move their bodies and/or being quieter than they would be in they felt safe to express themselves without judgement. These people are often in long term relationships with a partner who has a much lower libido or sex drive, than they do. But a number of them have been younger single people, afraid of being judged and unable to therefore find a partner.

It can be incredibly liberating to be slutty, which really just means unashamedly sexual, freely expressing desire and pleasure. Where long term couples have explored this through coaching/counselling and have opened up, being willing to be vulnerable with each other in a non-judgemental way, it has been life changing and relationship affirming.

If you are single or in any kind of relationship, it is worth really reflecting on how you feel and act when being sexually intimate. Are you authentic or are you holding back expressing your desires and/or your pleasure? Do you make others feel ashamed or bad for the way they express their desires and/or pleasure? Do you feel ashamed or bad for the way you would like to, do or have expressed your desires and/or pleasure?

Have you ever tried to open a conversation about something you desire only to have it shot down? Or been surprised by something someone asked and responded judgementally? I take pride in being non-judgemental, but I know that at times I judge myself and hold back, or I haven't been as kind as I could be when having that; 'cool that you like that, but it's not for me' conversation.

32

Inner Slut

Sara - *she/her*
I love my inner slut, this confident, highly sexual woman, comfortable in her own body around others. My inner slut knows exactly what she enjoys and one of those things is the sex equivalent of binge watching an entire Netflix series in a session. My inner slut can get very selfish, if this is mutually acceptable. If not, I work hard to ensure I focus on the person/people I am with, and not just myself.

33

Pleasure Dom & fucktoy

Lisa and Dr Mattel - *she/her & he/him*

I'm not exactly sure that Dr Mattel, a very very talented Pleasure Dom would describe me as a fucktoy for his amusement. We have never had that conversation. We set up the first play prior, with safety conversations and discussing limits etc. Dr Mattel is the only person I play with where I can turn up to an arranged play session and say "make me unable to think." and know he can provide more than I expected. I mean I probably could say that with one or two other people, who would understand what I am getting at, which is I want to be in my subspace, but without any effort on my behalf, and with handing over control from the very beginning.

Dr Mattel has possibly the largest collection of sex toys that I have ever seen, including those of a professional dominatrix in her private dungeon. And, more importantly, he knows how to use them to get the greatest pleasure for me, and I suspect everyone he plays with, as they all return with enthusiasm and knowledge their next session will be better than their last. Finally, he enjoys his play sessions as much as his play partners, without a need for penetrative play.

Just responding to a text message or sending one asking if we can meet up, is the stage at which my inner slut can be released. Driving there is a commitment to orgasm as much as he would like me to. To just give him the control of my body for as long as the session lasts. I do not do this with anyone else. I am not entirely sure why I trusted him on the spot when we met for that first discussion at a coffee shop. Maybe it was the total lack of pretentiousness, the calm confidence that oozed from him that he knew what he liked and knew how to have a lot of fun sexually without judgement. Dressed much more casually than most people I have met for coffee, he came across as sexually confident, kind and interesting as a person.

Pretty much my sexual turn on jackpot. I don't have a physical type. I am not sure if he does or not for his play. His relationships are nothing to do with me, but he talks about the women he loves with respect and genuine care. Big tick from me.

What I got and what I expected from that first play were two very different things. I wasn't sure if I would go back. This was a whole other level of slut than I was used to. And I wasn't sure if I could mentally handle it or not, no matter how pleasurable it had been, having tens of orgasms before he released me from the cuffs and ropes.

His after care was provided exactly as I had said I need. He checked in on me the next day by text. This was a true dom, one who knew how to play safely, sanely and consensually, with great skill and more pleasure than I have had in a very long time.

After the second play, where he more than doubled my number of orgasms from our previous session, with more of his vast range of toys and the addition of another woman, playing with me restrained blindfolded, so I wasn't sure who was doing what, I really wasn't sure I was going to go back. I had not played with another woman for over 3 years. Had not looked at another woman for over 3 years. Had not allowed myself to desire another woman, despite repeated requests for threesomes from various lovers and FWBs over those 3 years.

I had absolutely agreed to her joining in. I had one the shittiest days at work that I had had for a long time and I just wanted to get out of my head and into the pleasure that my body can experience. I am very grateful for all the contextual things that led to this play because one of the things that came out of it was that I have allowed myself to desire women again. I also allowed myself to just enjoy the play with Dr Mattel and accept that inner slut really likes to play with him and his toys. To be restrained and deprived sensorially as he chooses, to ask for changes or pauses in the play as and when I need or want to.

If I could clone his knowledge, skills and attitude to sexual pleasure and put it in the water, I would.

34

Pleasure Dom & slut

Paula - she/her, straight

When I get in that pleasure zone, of just being submissive and giving over control, I give in to that all encompassing pleasure. I forget to pay attention to anything, or rather I'm not capable of doing so as my whole body fills with ever increasing pleasure as each orgasm builds on the crescendo of the last one.

I hear the voice telling me not to cum and I both sigh with frustration and with pleasure. I feel the hand spanking my ass and my body moves with excitement and my pussy responds by getting even wetter.

I feel the hold, keeping me firmly in place and I melt into it, safe in my submission. When allowed, when told to cum, I cum hard and deep and exist just in those moments of pure pleasure.

What each Pleasure Dom understands by that title is individual. What they want and expect from the person or people that they play with can vary not just between Pleasure Dom's but also with each of their sexual partners too. This is why it is important to discuss openly and honestly with each person.

35

Honesty and Openness

Honesty and openness are highly erotic in all stages of play and relationships. These are not be confused with rudeness or unkindness. "I love a curvy woman with a soft belly," is honest and open and kind. "Wow you are fat" is unkind. "I haven't had as many sexual partners as you so I am nervous," is honest and open and kind. "You seem to be a bit of a whore" is rude.

I find honesty and openness erotic. It is the vulnerability. I don't care if you have had 1000 or 10 or no previous partners. I care about your self-care and sexual health. And I care about this whether we have a single play session, a short or long term FWB or a relationship. Whether these are kink or vanilla or a combo.

If you are open and honest in our negotiations about what we might want to do should we click when we meet, then I feel more comfortable sharing openly and honestly. If you lie, this is a big turn off. Admitting you are married after saying you are single tells me I cannot trust you. Sex is about trust.

Nina *- she/her, polysexual*

I am single but am open and honest about my regular FWBs and my ENM starting point. For some people this means I am not for them but that is fine. I do not need to fuck every person who turns me on. I do not need to be desired by every person I

115

come into contact with. But if I desire you, I will be open and honest with you about it. If I don't, I will also be honest about this.

The most erotic play is that which is based in openness and honesty. The potential play partner who says 'these are my hard limits' gives me permission to play in every other way. Knowing I can explore and play and play is such a turn on. There can be myriad hard limits and still I am wet with excitement about the things that can be done.

If you want tying up or restraining physically in any way, you need everyone involved to be open and honest. If you want impact play, you need the same. This is the only way to build trust. Breaking trust is breaking the mood, any turn on is gone. Building trust builds erotic sensation.

People worry about being judged, being perceived of as less than. They rarely worry about lying to prevent being judged. This means that one way to combat the very real toxic culture of lying within dating is for most people to be honest and open by default.

I can respect someone that puts married & poly, or ENM with primary partner on their profile. I cannot respect of trust someone who says they are divorced but in actuality is simply in the spare room of the marital home whilst deciding whether or not to separate or even worse is essentially in a committed monogamous relationship and lying to both their partner and any potential matches.

If you are honest about who you are and what you are looking for, it saves everyone a lot of time and wasted energy. There will be at least one, probably tens of people who are looking for what you are offering and who may well be compatible. We also need to accept that not everyone we fuck will want to see us again. Ghosting is pathetic though, none of us are kids, it is not hard to text or otherwise private message a 'thanks for that, but I think we are incompatible. Good luck finding what you are looking for.' Also, unless you are in a big city, people talk and after a while people who regularly ghost others may well find they struggle to get dates or hookups.

36

Effort

Kat - she/her, straight

I am picking you up tonight to play. When you get out of your car at our rendezvous, you look hot. You always look hot, but you dressed up really nicely. You look so sexy. When someone makes a little bit of effort for you, it is such a big turn on. I made an effort too. I wore the lace thong that you like so much and a dress with lots of access for you.

You paid so much attention to how my body was responding to your touch and your kisses. I could feel the effort you were putting in and that too was a turn on. You spread my legs gently but firmly. I thought about the last inspection, when I was on all fours legs spread, as requested, so my pussy and my ass could be inspected to see how much I wanted something inside me.

You kissed me as you played with my clit and my wet pussy, letting me know that this time I can let go of my control and you would take control. I relaxed into your firm, strong arms, making the effort to shift my language to please and thank you and to show and tell you when I am liking what you are doing or to ask, then beg to cum.

After you put so much effort into my after care, holding me close with a warm cuddle, gently kissing my head and stroking my back. I lay satiated in your arms. This we can do again.

ONSs and one off hookups are pretty much the only sex that it is ok not to bother putting much effort into. They still need to be safe, sane and consensual, but if you are never going to meet again, it really doesn't matter if you don't make much of an effort with what you wear, or how you play off each other.

Any other sexual intimacy, where you plan to see the person again or you have seen them previously, is vastly improved when everyone involved puts in at least some effort.

- Effort to be clean and smell good, whatever that means for the people involved
- Effort to communicate
- Effort to look sexy/desirable in the context of what you both/all like
- Effort to read and respond to the other person/people's desires
- Effort to express your pleasure

37

Contrasts

T - *she/her, bisexual*

Sometimes you kiss me so tenderly, making sure I know you get pleasure from my pleasure. At other times you flick your belt over my ass cheeks, the thwack signalling your pleasure and mine, whilst the feel of the building force shows me you care about my pleasure and my thanks and red ass giving you your pleasure.

Sometimes I kiss you from head to toe. Spending time enjoying the sensation of your skin in my mouth and the movements of your body building my pleasure at your pleasure. I love it when you arch into a kiss or moan softly. I love watching your cock get harder and harder without even being touched.

Sometimes you restrain my wrists or legs with your powerful arms and hands making sure I can't wiggle away. At other times, I sit on you, riding your cock as I lean forward, each of my hands wrapped around one of your wrists, my body weight keeping you in place more than my strength. I love the vulnerability that you have when restrained like this, submissive and asking me to please take control.

Oftentimes I give you back the control before you orgasm, but not always. Just depends on my mood, your mood and the interaction of desire and patience. If I have edged you without enough skill you need to take the control back but if I have edged you perfectly, you aren't capable of asking for or even desiring control back.

I am looking for the person that can take me to that place of submission that you think is typical but is actually quite rare. It takes a combination of skill, trust, safety and presence of mind. Domination in this kind of play requires minute adjustments to keep the submissive safe and secure and oh so turned on that they cannot think for themselves but feel so safe that they feel good about this.

I am not sure why I do not submit to you in this way. Certainly, you are still building your skills, but you are a fast learner and I trust you in play. Perhaps it is that you do not show me the presence of mind that I show you in domination. Perhaps it is that I am more dom than sub and I won't let go for anyone. Who knows.

Many people do not realise that they can and may want to express themselves sexually, very differently within different contexts or with different people. Some of the most rewarding first sexual catchups have been with people who ask questions;

- How do you cum best?
- What kinds of things turn you on?
- Is this nice?
- Can you show me, how you like to be touched?

Sexual confidence in combination with kindness is the combination that makes me feel I have hit the jackpot with in a potential FWB or play partner or partner. As a society we find it hard to differentiate between sexual confidence and arrogance, between kindness and being perceived to be a pushover. Humans are complex beings with contrasting characteristics.

Think about what it is that you find sexually attractive in a person, not physically but emotionally, in terms of personality. How does that compare and contrast with your authentic personality?

RJ - she/her, straight

I am quite naturally bossy and like to take charge in my everyday life. This contrasts with my social anxiety in non-sexual settings and with my submissive play.

Being reflective and becoming more comfortable with your own personality contrasts, enables you to be more authentic and open. Which in turn facilitates the potential for more pleasure during sex.

38

Kindness in Kink

Juliet - she/her, switch

Whether I am being a submissive or a Dom I like to play with kindness. A tender kiss before or after play. Edging to increase pleasure not to be mean.

Saying you are a dom is not an excuse to just take pleasure and inflict pain on your terms for you with no consideration for the other. Saying you are submissive does not mean you are worthless and should not be considered.

We fuck or we submit or we Dom or we have sex or we make love, all of these are about human connection and human pleasure. Being really kind does not mean you cannot sub or dom or fuck around.

Being a mean shit does mean you shouldn't dom. You shouldn't inflict your cruelty on others while pretending you give a shit about them and their pleasure.

Over the last few years I have noticed a worrying trend within the kink community, where people new to the community play with no knowledge or understanding of the structure, communication and consent levels required for safe, sane and consensual kink play. As a result, people are getting emotionally damaged and physically hurt.

Young adults who should be able to explore safely are deepening their sexual trauma through uninformed consent that is neither safe nor sane to high level impact play that takes no account of their mental or physical state. Adults are risking financial and personal ruin to indulge in fetishes or kinks that are illegal.

Kindness underscores safe, sane and consensual. Kindness to self and kindness to the others involved.

Dinah - *she/her, bisexual*

I felt like kissing today. And licking. Slow gentle kisses, the type where the lips only just touch the skin. Licking that is only just licking, my tongue moving over your body without touching the skin, instead I am really licking your soft body hairs.

Where you shaved, there my tongue slowly moves over your skin. I alternate between kissing and licking. It took me long enough to persuade you to get out of the water and lay down naked so I could kiss you all over. You had just wanted my mouth on your cock. Whereas I wanted to taste you all over, to feel you with my lips and my tongue.

Finally you lay down and I asked you to lay on your side, one leg bent so that I have full access to all of you. So beautiful, I traced my lips and my tongue from your neck to your feet and back. Slowly, so slowly, with more time spent licking and kissing in places you had not thought of as erogenous before. I love turning you on like this.

When I asked where you liked it the most, you said everywhere, you said you'd forgotten about your cock, that you were just enjoying me enjoying you. Then you said you were in a kissing mood and you flipped me over onto my back and spread my legs. You never kiss my pussy, but ohhhh you got so close. It made me think you never have, never kissed anyone's pussy. I forget how inexperienced you are.

You kissed my belly as you slid your fingers into my pussy and asked if you could have the hard toy. You have been waiting a while for me to let you play with my new hard toys, waiting until I was more submissive than dominant. I passed you both toys and said, only one at a time. I know which one you really wanted to play with, but I really wanted to play with the other.

We played with both, one and then the other. You found the rose sexy, I should have asked for a picture, you said the black rose looked so beautiful sitting just outside me, the rest of the toy inside. But you enjoyed the glass dildo as much as I did. You could feel it inside me whilst you were fucking me too, your hard cock so much softer than the solid glass. I came so hard I couldn't hold the dildo anymore and so you were filling me with your fingers and your cock until we both came hard and intensely. All this from a gentle kiss.

Everyone starts out inexperienced. Experience is not an age thing. It is an opportunity to explore and play, thing. You can be incredibly experienced with one partner and lack experience more generally. Being deliberately gently can be a beautiful way to start sexual intimacy with someone who is not very experienced, as well as just being erotic in general.

Gently exploring someone's body may be the first time they have ever really been present and able to focus on their pleasure. What feels good where. Dinah shared how this particular partner had never given a woman oral sex, and it was not something he was comfortable exploring. He was comfortable being adventurous in other ways but this comfort largely stemmed from her taking the time early on in their sexual relationship, to explore his body gently.

39

Stay Still Until

Lila - she/her, straight
Sitting astride him, riding his hard cock I could feel his tiredness from a long hard day. I wanted to gift him a massive whole of body releases orgasm. I held one of each of his hands in mine and placed them above his head. Leaning forward slightly, all my weight was on his hands, making an effective restraint.

I whispered in his ear, "don't move, just stay still" as I continued to ride his cock, deep and hard. As his moans increased, I licked up his neck to his ear and gentled nibbled that. He moved his head, and I reminded him to stay still. He moved his head again mid moan so I slowed my movements right down. I slowly slowly moved my soaking wet pussy up and down the length of his cock.

"Stay still," I whispered in his ear, "until you can't stand it anymore and you need to take control. When that happens take your hands back and take the control." I love that look, where not just the eyes, but the whole body respond with desire. I could see his desire building and building.

I alternated a few long but slow and gentle caresses of his cock with my pussy with deep hard and fast movements where my ass slammed into his legs and my clit into his lower abdomen. He felt me cum, gasping and moaning that I had just got even wetter. I continued to ride his cock and kiss his neck and earlobes.

Changing my angle very slightly his moans increased in intensity as the desire in his eyes and his restricted body movements demonstrated. I reminded him to stay still unless he was needed to take control. He pulled his hands free and holds me tightly so that he was controlling how deep and fast and hard he was thrusting. We both started to cum, long, loud and hard. His whole body shuddering under mine as he continued to hold me tight. I could feel his cock throbbing with each aftershock of his huge orgasm, our combined cum dripping down my thigh.
Our bodies relaxed into each other, and we lay relaxed entwined, wet and satiated for the moment.

Not all sex can result in a both/all people having orgasms at the same time. There can be immense social pressure for this to happen. Pressure on people of all genders. It really doesn't matter if you cum at the same time or not, or even if you cum at all – if you are ok with or even desire to not cum.

What is important is for everyone's desire and pleasure to be thought about and acted on respectfully, consensually. In this particular interaction, Lila had not been dominant with this partner before, but the sex they had had indicated to Lila that her partner would be open to this. They had a very open communication style and were comfortable discussing what they liked and did not like and providing feedback on pleasure during sex.

When Lila initially whispered in her partner's ear, "don't move, just stay still", she knew if he did not want to stay still, he would have said no and they just would have shifted our dynamic back to how it normally was. This partner was used to physically restraining Lila with his hands and is significantly stronger that Lila. So, Lila knew that holding his hands above his head was not something that he could not have changed if he did not like.

Lila also shared the look on her partner's face as she restrained his wrists with her hands. Lila described the look as one of pure lust and that following this his body moved towards and into hers with obvious desire.

Paula *- she/her, submissive/slut*

My pleasure dom (for slut) will use verbal restraint, telling me to stay still, knowing full well I cannot. For us, this leads to him spanking me and me thanking him.

My pleasure dom (for fucktoy) physically restrains me, knowing it turns me on, but is also not massively effective if I wriggle too much. I possibly owe him for some broken ropes. One of his other fucktoys noted that I was the reason he uses chains now for restraint!

40

50 Shades

I didn't read the book. It didn't interest me, too much of a cliché. I watched the movie last night because I was bored, had nothing better to do and it was downloaded and I had rubbish Wi-Fi and no phone coverage. Firstly there wasn't any sex shown.... The average Hollywood blockbuster has more obvious representations of sex and with the amount of free porn available, they really could have done better.

But now I understand why so many people think all kink is about owning another person and controlling them 24/7 (or being controlled by them 24/7). Yes, for some people that is what they want and enjoy, but for most people, paying the mortgage somewhat takes up some of that time.

Anna - *she/her*

I don't know if the book and the movie were the same but I was so disappointed in the portrayal of whipping. There is a skill in whipping to maximise pleasure, that was not what was shown. A beautiful whip can also be so much more than just a line across a body. It can tease and caress, excite and ignite.

And yes I can count each lash, but oh so much more pleasurable to count and thank the person, genuinely meaning it as they bring the whip down specifically to heighten both of our pleasure. If I am being whipped as a pun-

ishment there is little doubt that I deliberately needed to be punished. Craving that feel of leather on skin, but done in ways that make me wetter and wetter. That lead to that look in my eyes that says, 'ok. I give you the control fully now, please bring us both intense pleasure.' A whip can be used to tease a clit and pussy in so many ways....

I bought a belt today. I picked each one up feeling it with both my hands. Running my hand over both the hard and the soft leather side. Thinking about the weight and the width and if this belt was the right one or not. The one I bought has an easy release, but one you can hear as hearing a belt being undone and then removed is an amazing sensation. Waiting for it to be raised and brought down.... And then when it is, instant wet. Instant ache. Instant desire. Of course I want to say thank you for all of that. The skill is to keep that response and not tip over into pure pain without the pleasure.

Different weights of belts need different levels of force to ensure maximise pleasure for both people, with those beautiful pink lines often having the same impact on a play partner as the feel of the leather warming up my ass cheeks has on me. I hope I picked the right belt, if it is perfect sometimes I can cum just from that.

There are a lot of safety considerations in impact play. What is used for the impact, how it is used, how much force and where the impact is. Pain releases endorphins, which are happy chemicals, so it can be easy to exceed a submissive's limits without them realising it until after the play when their body is physically damaged beyond what is safe and sane.

Everyone should have personal limits around impact play for both receiving and giving. Limits can range from not at all, through no blood, no open wounds, no welts and no bruising to welts and bruising being fine. I am not judging people that desire to receive or give welts and bruising. I understand the sexual high that can come from these, they are just not for everyone.

No matter whether impact play is light or hard, certain parts of the body should not be struck, whilst others should always have less force to prevent permanent damage. You want to whip, paddle or spank areas on the body that have a good layer of fat on them to protect the body. The safest areas are the buttocks/ass and thighs. You never want to land an impact on someone's spine. You want to avoid whipping or any other impact on the lower back where the kidneys are. Avoid any areas in which you could damage organs.

A good visual chart of safe zones for impact play is available for free download from:

https://www.devianceanddesire.com/wp-content/uploads/2014/12/BDSMImpactSafeZones_121117.pdf

41

Out in the Bush

Walking through the bush to get to the beach today, there were some perfect outdoor sex spots. Totally hidden from the footpath but reasonably easy to access. I was by myself so instead of taking advantage of these spots I just reminisced about some of the great sex I've had in the bush.

Bush sex is very dependent on what there is to hold onto and at what height. Will she get to sit on a tree branch or bend over holding onto a fence post? When there is totally nothing to hold onto is the ground okay to sit/lie/kneel on? Or is the Ute going to be the thing to hold onto/lie on/in?

It's always so erotic to be surrounded by beautiful plants and hear the birds and ocean or stream whilst fucking hard and fast. Cumming intensified by the possibility that someone might hear or see. Ummmm so many options....

I have been having outdoor sex since my first sexual experiences as a teen, both my first girlfriend and my first boyfriend introduced me to this, and I assumed that it was something everyone did! As a teen and young adult, I took far more risks around public sex than I do now.

Many people have fantasies about sex in places other than their bed! It is quite normal to imagine or fantasise about lots of different scenarios. Some people like outdoor or nature sex and the thing they enjoy is being in a natural outdoor setting; beach, garden, bush etc. For others the outdoor sex is about exhibitionism, a desire to be seen or the risk of being seen. This needs to be balanced with the risk of breaking the law for indecent exposure (in a public place), which is where the bush is safer as you are so unlikely to encounter someone else!

If you are an exhibitionist, then private sex parties are a safe way to 'be on display' to others who want to watch. It is not ok to force others who are not into watching to watch, which can happen in public places! It is also illegal to have your naked genitals on display in public in many places.

Bear in mind that some people like their fantasies to stay just that, a fantasy. Whilst other people would really like to live out their fantasies, to bring them to life. If a sexual partner shares their fantasies with you, ask them if they would like this to come to life, or if they want to keep this one as a fantasy only.

42

Fantasy

Vickie - *she/her*

We meet after work, both still dressed in work clothes. You look smart and professional which I find sexy. I am wearing a smart casual wrap around dress with a lacy G-string underneath and no bra. You can slide your hand through the side of the dress and around to caress my ass and feel the bare cheeks with lace between.

I lean in to give you a kiss but continue to kiss slowly down your neck to your shirt collar. I reach up and start to unbutton your shirt so I can kiss your body and suck and bite your nipples. I undo your pants and slide them down, continuing to kiss and bite and lick everywhere except your cock. That I am playing with, using my hands and fingers to find out just how you want you cock touching today. I caress your cock ring, and kiss just above your groin over and over. Insistent kisses.

You undo my dress and start to rub and pull and pinch my nipples. When they are hard and pink you take them into your mouth one at a time to suck and kiss and bite, deciding how hard to bite by the tone of my moans. You pull my dress off and each hand traces one of my ass cheeks.

Your hands move and I hold myself totally still for a second, both antici-pating and hoping for a spank. Instead, you ask me to turn around and bend over so that you can see how wet I am. As I bend, you tell me to pinch my nipples, which makes me even wetter, as you can clearly tell from the very wet small strip of cloth covering my pussy.

You ask me what I want, and I tell you that I really want to feel your tongue on my clit and your fingers in my pussy. That every time I think about you doing that, I get wet. You tell me to take the rest of my clothes off and lie down with my legs spread and my knees bent to expose as much of me as possible. I do. You just look for a while. Whilst I wait. The waiting is making me ache inside. Then I feel your tongue flick across my clit and around my pussy lips. My body both arches and melts.

I remember how good your beautiful glass flower dildo felt inside me and my body arches up to meet your tongue. You tell me that if I can't stay still you will need to restrain me. And then you push your tongue into my pussy and I arch my back, moaning and then saying thank you. When you stop and look up you ask if the thank you was for the restraints or for the pleasure your tongue was giving me. Your eyes show you are laughing but your tone is serious.

I say 'both' quietly as you restrain me with legs wide apart and hands spread out, the fur lined cuffs comfortable but effectively preventing me from moving more than a tiny amount. Having put a pillow under my ass, I am very exposed for you and clearly very wet.

You go back to licking and sucking and occasionally gently biting my clit then pushing your tongue into my increasing wetness. One of your fingers is tracing my wetness down from my pussy around and then into my tight ass. You tease me by circling your finger around and around as I try to move my ass towards it but can't. "Please" I ask. "Please."

"Please what?" Is your response. "Please fuck me. Please. Anywhere. Please. With your tongue or your fingers or one of your toys." I plead. I think about how the glass dildo slid inside me so easily and as I pushed it in and pulled it out, the bumps on the outside felt so good, making me ache with desire. You push a finger into my now wet ass, through the first tight muscles and to the second. You play with my ass whilst you continue to lick and suck my pussy. "Thank you," I whisper.

You stop. I whimper and you run your wet fingers over my nipples. Then you very deliberately slowly suck and lick my nipples until I cry out with need and desire.

I haven't been restrained for such a long time and I can't work out if I want to fight the restraints or relax into them. Just thinking is hard as my desire is so intense. I want so badly to have something inside my pussy and something inside my ass.

You hold up two dildos so I can see them and you ask me to pick one, the left or the right. One is much bigger than the other/ but I don't know how or where you are planning to use it nor on who. Plus, frustratingly for me I am struggling to think, so I just choose right in the hope it will be right. You look delighted that I choose the smaller of the two and you slowly rub lube all over it. Rubbing it down to the base, carefully ensuring the head is covered generously. "Ready?"

You spread my cheeks by holding them with your hands between the pillow and my ass. I gasp as you start to push the dildo into my ass. It is silicone and that soft hard that feels so good. I try to move against the restraints and onto the dildo. You push it all the way in and then leave it, going back to licking my clit and pussy. I am soaking wet; the wetness is dripping down my ass cheeks and coating my open thighs.

My pussy aches and my clit is so close to cumming. You move your mouth away and hold up the glass flower dildo asking me how much I want it. My eyes betray me, and you demand that I tell you. I do, "I want it so much, I want to feel it inside my pussy now, please, please."

Though in all honesty at this point I just want to be fucked however you want until I cum. I want you to unrestrain me so I can fuck the dildo in my ass whilst you fuck my pussy with whatever you choose. I need to feel filled. You slide that beautiful flower in as far as it goes and pull it out again. I relax into the restraints and moan loudly. As you continue to move the glass dildo in and out of my aching pussy you vary the pace and rhythm to see what makes me moan with what tone and what volume. You move the flower that sits on the end of the glass dildo so that my g-spot is being hit over and over again. I can feel the orgasm building, my ass full and my pussy tightly gripping the glass flower as you push and pull repeatedly.

"Don't cum," you say. I whisper "ok," almost crying with frustration. You pinch my nipples and kiss my mouth and slap the bottom of the dildo in my

ass. It pushes in slightly further and bounces back out halfway. "Ohhhh." I hadn't expected that, and it was nice. Very nice. The glass flower is resting in my pussy as you slap the base of the dildo in my ass over and over. "Don't cum. Tell me when to stop," you say.

"Uhhh uhhh ohhh stop please." You do one more slap to see if I can control myself. I did. "Good girl," you say as you undo my wrist restraints and tell me to fuck myself with the glass dildo with one hand and play with my clit with the other. You pull the dildo out of my ass and put a condom on your hard cock. You push two fingers around my pussy lips making them wet and add that wetness to the lube you just covered the condom with.

"Stop touching," you say, and I stop immediately, holding both hands still. "Spread your cheeks for me," you command. I put my hands under my ass and spread it as wide apart as I can.

Your cock teases me initially and then fills my ass. You tell me to, "Continue to play with your clit now, pinch and pull it. You can choose how hard or soft."

"Thank you," I murmur. "Fuck yourself too. But don't come yet. You need to ask if you can come," you state in that tone of voice that suggests there is no other option. Your cock fills my ass. it feels so good as you move it in and out, deep and thrusting but gentle enough that it is pure pleasure and no pain. The flower feels so good and my clit is so hard.

I forget to ask and start to cum. You tell me to stop, and I do. I apologise and you tell me that you will punish me later. I feel the excitement build further and I know when you let me cum it is going to be a huge explosion of wetness from both of us. You deny me orgasm a couple more times and then correctly read that I have totally lost control and am being driven by desire and pleasure.

"Cum now," you command, as I cum intensely from my clit, my pussy and my ass. The feel of your cock throbbing as you orgasm in my ass heightens my pleasure and my orgasmming ass tightly grips your cock intensifying the sensations for both of us.

Vickie told me that this is a common fantasy for her. It is one that she personally is happy to bring to life. For many people, the idea of anything anal may be fine as fantasy but is not ok in real life. Orgasm control is also something that some play within real life, both denying, being denied and being told when to cum.

Some people really enjoy playing with orgasm edging or control/denial, whilst for others this can be frustrating and/or annoying and totally off putting.

43

Control

*C***hloe** *- she/her, bisexual, switch*
In vanilla life I like to be in control. I am decisive, logical and firm but fair. In my kinky sex life, I like to flow from in control of myself to not, from controlling another to giving them the control, to switch. After a day of being in charge, sometimes I want to just give all the control to someone else. I don't want to think or to make decisions. I can only do this with someone I know and trust. But when I do, I can totally let go and abandon myself and become immersed in the pleasures of the moment.

Tell me what to wear, where to meet you. Where to go next and how to position myself for you. Require me to follow your instructions if you want me to play with myself or hold myself open for you. Control when and how I can cum. Decide for me if I can have a number of small orgasms or keep building me up to a massive whole-body orgasm that leaves me curled up in a tiny ball needing your strong, warm embrace.

Control whether my legs are closed or open, whether my ass and pussy are exposed or covered, whether you fuck me with your tongue, fingers, cock and or toys. Take me out to dinner after you have inserted a vibrating toy in my pussy. Control the speed of the vibrations. As we eat, control how I can express my sexual excitement and ask me to describe my wetness to you.

Your control is guided by desire. Desire for your own pleasure but also desire to lead me to that place of total surrender where I cannot control my whole of body orgasm and my wetness drips down my thighs, and I hold on to your body so tight. Sometimes, if you are not feeling like controlling me, you will tease and tease me until I am so aroused and frustrated that I switch into being controlling and I lead you to where I want you and I put your fingers into my pussy and tell you exactly how I want you to fuck me whilst I play with and kiss and lick and bite you.

After a couple of quick orgasms, I will be aching for your cock and move so that I am sitting over you. I will lower myself onto you and fuck you so slowly until you beg for harder, deeper, faster. I don't give you what you want yet because I so love to see that sexual ache in your body and face. Once I have seen enough of your building desire, I fuck you how you like it, hard deep thrusts where I ride your cock so that it fills my pussy deeply and then I pull off so that only the very tip of your cock is still just inside me, slippery with my wetness. I slam my pussy back down, our bodies colliding with a loud slap of flesh on flesh. I make you cum as I keep riding you, I slip my hand around your balls alternately stroking and slapping them until you are losing control, and I can feel you exploding inside me.

Control can be around who controls the movement, how hard, how deep etc. It can be all encompassing or be a tiny part of the session. Some people like to be in control all of the time, in and out of 'sex'. Other people like to give up the control, others can't even conceive of these concepts. Others switch. There is no right or wrong. However, all control play NEEDS to be safe, sane and consensual. Coercion or any other way of taking or forcing control without full informed prior consent is abusive.

44

That Moment

 **M**aya - *she/her*

I had dinner with friends. They are a couple but they each know quite different sides to me. The woman and I met for an hour before he had finished teaching his fitness class.

We are relaxed and friendly. Excited to see each other and catch up on life. We talk rapidly, falling silent when he briefly enters the room. We sit close enough to touch but not touching. We are talking about sex but there is no sexual chemistry between us. We are friends with no sexual interest in one another.

She asks how I can have sex every day if it isn't exhausting. I laugh because I might sleep well after good sex, but I will happily have more in the middle of the night and the next morning. Clearly, we experience sex totally differently.

She has to go home to her kids before I am ready to leave. He and I sit and eat cake together. He drinks a second beer. This is notable because he doesn't usually drink, and it is a work night. When I get up to leave, he says he will walk me out. We hug and as he steps back, in that moment there is a shift. He looks me up and down, undressing me with his eyes and says, you look good. All of you looks good. I choose to ignore the clear signals because I know they are in theory monogamous, and I like them both too much to throw a spammer in the works.

He doesn't know I have a black lace g- string on under my leggings. That my pussy has made my G-string wet, not because of him but because I was thinking about some amazing sex, I had a few weeks ago and wondering if I will get to play with that guy again. I was thinking today what it would be nice to do again and what he or I or both of us would want to do differently.

My friend and I hug again, a lingering hug on his part. I lean into the hug and hug him tight back. "Night," I say. I drive off thinking about the amazing sex and wondering if it was as good for the guy as it was for me. My G-string so wet as I remember moments in time that my leggings are wet now too.

As an aside, this should NOT have happened. The male friend is an ass-hole. His girlfriend is amazing. And I do not ever, ever, ever, fuck with my friends' sexual partners or spouses.

Like some people, I rarely know when people are flirting with me, just not something I pick up on. One of the few cues I do pick up on is that up and down look, where you are being undressed with their eyes. I prefer less subtle cues, like saying; "wanna fuck." I accept this is a bit much for some people, but it is clear and leaves no room for assumptions and miscommunication.

I am like this because I mainly lived in shared accommodation with men who were upfront about who they liked and what they wanted to do. One of my long-term girlfriends once was horrified when I asked her if she wanted to have sex. Her face was a picture. She did though! I am not suggesting this works for everyone, and it can be offensive and too upfront. Instead, if meeting organically in person you can say things like.

"It was great meeting you; I'd love to get to know you better over coffee" or a walk or whatever seems appropriate.

"Hi, my name is Jo. I really like your outfit/music/hair (or whatever). Where did you get it?" This latter simply being a conversation starter.

Online people are more upfront and 'wanna fuck' is less offensive, but only if their profile makes it clear they are up for casual sex. If they are seeking a relationship, you should only be asking to meet not asking for sex. Nor should you be sending dick pics, or any other explicit pics and you should not be asking for explicit pics either.

Explicit pics should only be sent after asking if the person would like to see those pics. Do not expect pics in return.

It always amazes me when someone does post a pic online, when they have not checked for the identifying items in the background of the pic. Nude woman on the bed, pic of her kids on the nightstand… Dick pic in work bathroom, company logo visible in mirror. Dildo in ass shot with very distinctive tattoo legs in shot. Fine if you work in a job where this kind of thing is totally acceptable, but all over the world people have lost their jobs because their employer doesn't appreciate this kind of behaviour in staff.

Paisley *- she/her, straight*

Sometimes I am happy to receive pics, and at other times I am not. I never send them though. Been burned once and that is enough. There is someone out there reflecting on the threats of one very angry woman as to what will happen if he ever shares the screenshots he has.

45

Release

*A**nna** - she/her*
I'm both bored and overly busy. I hate be-
ing bored; I tend to do ridiculously uninhibited
things to break the boredom. Busy is good but overly
busy with the mundane is not. This leads to frustra-
tion and annoyance from which I seek release. The combination of lack of
inhibition and needing release is an interesting one.

An ex-FWB wanted to hang out when I was in this combination. We were
still friends, just not with benefits much anymore. He was clearly horny, or
as he would say, on on. In this mood he is often a selfish lover, his sole goal
being to cum, regardless of my pleasure. If I tease him right though, I can
get him to focus on my pleasure for long enough that I get to orgasm at least
twice before we cum together.

When we got in the car, he was a little shy and uncertain. He is never
sure these days if I will consent to fucking or not. His cock was not being shy,
or uncertain, and was definitely wanting attention.
I like to play, so I slipped my hand down his pants and started to play with
his cock and balls. I love the different textures on a hard cock, tracing my
fingers over each texture and using touch lightly and firmly to tease him un-
til he wants so much that he starts to give. His balls were so firm, and I know
he loves the possibility of being seen by other drivers going past. His cock so
hard under my fingers.

Pulling off the road, he drove down a dirt track a little way and parked. He took his clothes off and shifted over to my side of the car, positioned above me. "You have too many clothes on," his not-so-subtle comment, which means I want to fuck now. I was wet already anyway so I took my underwear off, leaving my dress in place. He wanted access to my nipples though, so he pulled the dress up to above my breasts and took a nipple into his mouth.

He pushed his cock deep inside my wet pussy and fucked me deep and hard as his mouth played with my nipple, teeth and tongue caressing, rubbing and biting, making my pussy wetter and wetter. My moans increased in volume and got closer and closer together as he continued to fuck me deep and hard. His breathing indicating his pleasure and the sensation of his cock throbbing showing me how close he is to cumming.

I shift slightly so as he pushes deep into me, my clit gets banged onto by his torso, my pleasure building. Sometimes I cum quietly the first time and only let him know the second or third or more time. This is one of those times. The raw release building and building until my pussy erupts with pleasure and I feel a total sense of release.

He isn't there yet and as he starts to cum, I cum again, loudly this time, holding onto his legs with mine, his sides with my hands as his hands grasp my shoulders and he fucks the last few strokes as deep and hard as possible. The release is awesome, my whole body relaxes, and my mind empties of everything except the sensation of my final orgasm.

I am an incredibly lucky woman. I am multi-orgasmic and can cum from a multitude of different touches on different parts of my body. I am very aware that this is not something that everyone experiences, and indeed that for some people my ability to cum over and over is very off putting. I do not play with these people more than three times.

For people with a penis, most can only cum one or maybe two times in any sex session, unless they are using Viagra or a similar drug. A few can, but not many. For people with a vagina and clitoris, it is a lot more variable. People who are comfortable with anal stimulation of any kind, tongue, fingers, toys etc, can usually orgasm from the stimulation. Vaginal stimulation/penetration may or may not lead to orgasm, with some people never orgasming from penis or sex toy inside their vagina.

Getting to orgasm usually requires both feeling emotionally and psychologically safe as well as having pleasurable physical sensations. Even with all of these three an orgasm can be elusive for many people occasionally.

How that lack of orgasm, or indeed any lack of hard on or wetness, are managed will significantly impact things going forward. Performance anxiety is real for people of any gender.

46

Waiting

 *- she/her, submissive*

Waiting in the car I check my phone. I'm still five minutes early. I've parked around the corner from the café so that my car won't be seen outside it by anyone. Just in case they wonder what I am doing here. Somewhere I don't normally come or cum. He had asked me not to wear underwear, so I hadn't. I felt exposed and aroused even though unless I spread my legs very wide, my dress was long enough to provide a modicum of modesty.

I got up, locked the car and went over to the cafe.

I wasn't sure if he would be here yet and I couldn't remember if I was meant to meet him inside or outside. Just as I was about to text, I heard my name. I turned to say yes. As soon as I had uttered the word, quick as lightning his hand reached up under my skirt to do a quick check that I really wasn't wearing anything else. "Good girl" he said. "I think this going to be fun, let's go and sit down."

He indicated I should sit in a booth as he sat next to me. "Are you happy for me to play" he asked. I nodded and let out a breathy yes. "Ok, but you have to eat and drink as if I am not touching you. If you squirm or make noise I'll stop, ok?" Another nod. And a small squeak that was meant to be yes. He ordered a large milkshake for me and some ice cream. Not the dinner I had been expecting but one I would enjoy anyway.

While we were waiting, he told me to spread my legs wider and pull my dress up at the front, so my pussy was exposed for him when he turned his head and looked down. No one else would be able to see but he could. He lay his hand on my lap so that his fingertips were sitting on my lips. He spread my lips. The milkshake and ice cream arrived. He told me to start eating and drinking. He took a spoon of ice cream and lowered it down onto my open pussy lips.

It was cold against my hot wetness, and I nearly jumped. But I wanted to be a good girl, so I just ate another spoonful of the ice-cream. He played with the ice-cream on me until it melted on and in me. His fingers pushed deeper inside. I could feel him moving them towards my g-spot. I wondered how messy this was going to get and knew I could not ever come back here without blushing.

My face must have turned red because he asked me if I wanted him to stop. He held his two fingers totally still inside me. "Please don't stop," I asked. "Why not" was his response...

That night ended up in some very very hot sex. In a much less public setting.

As a word of advice, if you are going to be having sex in any 'public areas' check for security cameras! Play like this needs to be set up to not offend people who may not want to see this kind of thing and to ensure you don't end up getting arrested for public indecency. Different layouts of cafes etc can lead to some very unintended flashing. Of which I have been on the receiving end, and it is a tad weird and a bit uncomfortable. To look or not to look?

Was at a DJ event with a friend. We were chilling for a bit. The VIP area behind us. I turned to get something out of my bag and a woman sitting in the VIP area was wearing a very short skirt and a thong that did not cover her at all, and everything was highly visible. I was uncomfortable because I wasn't sure if she was meaning to flash everyone or not. If she wasn't wearing underwear, I probably would have been more comfortable. Not that it was her job to make me comfortable, but I personally don't want to assume consent for everyone around, and it is unethical and not consensual to involve non-consenting others for your own kicks/sexual satisfaction.

47

On Mute, Camera Off

*L**una** - she/her, straight*
*   I am meant to be working but I'm horny. My pussy is wet and aching and my knickers are getting wetter. I can't leave the computer as I have a zoom meeting in a few minutes. I sign in and type the usual excuse in the chat box before anyone else gets into the meeting. 'Sorry internet is rubbish again, have to have my camera off but I'm here.' Then I mute my mic. The problem is I take the minutes of the meeting so I know I may need to have the mic on to check things.*

This means I am going to have to be very quiet with my masturbation. I usually play on my phone when I am on zoom; helps keep me awake. And during the last zoom I'd be sent a video that really turned me on. Normally I prefer written erotica to filmed like, but I'd got pretty wet with this one. The guy who sent it to me knows me well. He had also messaged to dare me to masturbate whilst on my next work zoom call.

I make sure my phone is on mute, and I open up the saved webpage of a guy edging this woman just using his fingers until she can hardly stand it, then he adds a vibrator. Alternating it between her clit and her pussy. I play it on silent and pull my dress up and push my hand down my knickers. I play with my clit for a few seconds but my pussy aches I want something in it and my fingers are right there and won't make a noise. This is important

159

as one of my colleagues is always asking what the noises are in people's backgrounds.

I'm frustrated, I want fingers on my clit and in my pussy. I look at the screen, certain I can leave for a minute at least to go get my littlest dildo. I open the bedside drawer and pull my knickers to the side and sink the dildo in as far in as it will go. I sigh quietly and hook the knickers back in place, so they hold the dildo in place while I walk back to my desk in time to catch my name.

I quickly turn the mic on to respond and with my other hand I start playing with my clit, rubbing wetness from my soaking wet pussy up and around and over my clit. The dildo sits deeply inside me. And I can make it move slightly in and out by rocking my body back and forth on my chair as I play with my growing clit. Good job my camera is off.

My knickers are soaking, and the intensity is building. With one hand I am still typing the minutes as with the other I am bringing myself to orgasm and trying not to moan out loud, being as quiet as I can.

One of the subreddits I am active in had a whole series of posts about mainly men masturbating whilst on work zooms/teams meetings. One of the guys asked if any women in the threads had played with themselves whilst working online. Made me reflect on this dare.

Yes, I came. Was it hot? Maybe, but also maybe not! Probably hotter for someone else reading about it, than me actually doing it. Have I done it again? No.... But I have had sex with someone else whilst the camera and mic were off. Not the best soundtrack to fuck to, but he thought it was super hot. Which meant he was really turned on, so it was only a quick fuck.

Please make sure to either keep this as a fantasy OR if you do try this in real life, ensure the microphone is on MUTE and the camera is OFF or you are liable to be unemployed very soon, unless of course you are selling sexual content online. In which case enjoy but try to stay safe!

48

Wet

Nina - she/her
Being wet and waiting is a beautiful place to be. Waiting for someone or something to touch my clit or sink deep into my wet and waiting pussy. So many ways to get me wet and so many ways to keep me waiting.

Sometimes I get so wet just from talking or texting that my knickers are totally soaked. Other times I am lucky to being teased in person. To be teased with words and with touch. Touch that gets close but does not touch. Or touch that lightly flicks or gently drags the whip across my open pussy to get my clit even more excited.

I love to be so wet I ache for any kind of touch on my clit and in my pussy. To drip down my thighs before I have had anything inside me.

Sexual desire is messy, sex is messy. Wet and sticky. This is something that sex ed never talks about. Precum oozes or drips from a penis. Wetness coats labia and slowly drips down the tops of thighs. Cum adds to the wet sticky mess. Some people are really not ok with this, whilst others revel in the smells, textures and tastes. Find out what your likes and dislikes are, what turns you on and what does not. Then talk to anyone you have sex with and find out what they like.

One guy I know loves to cover his female partners' lips and ass with lube, no matter how wet they already are, and despite not actually engaging in anal play. Another man I know doesn't like to use lube at all. Some of the people I know talk about enjoying the differences between the taste and feel of their wetness versus someone else's, using their tongue and fingers to touch themself before the other person, then back to themself.

49

Touch

Anna - she/her

It was the gentlest kiss, so light my lips barely touched the tip of his sleeping cock. My hair draped over his torso as I leaned down and across and back up. The lightest kiss with the tiniest lick. My tongue feeling the velvety tip and my lips feeling the silky-smooth skin at the end of his cock.

Sometimes it is the firmest touch that turns him on. When I grab hold on his side with my whole hand or my mouth sinks into his side so that it is filled with his firm flesh before I twist away and plant firm kisses up and down his torso. Playing with the different feels of lick, kiss and stroke.

This is really what turns me on the most, playing with touch. Exploring another's body with my lips, tongue and fingers. Seeing their body react to the different types of touch on different parts of their body. I am not sure why people don't all spend more time exploring touch. It is both incredibly selfish and incredibly connecting. I love the feeling of their body through my touch, the selfish, and I love reading their responses to heighten their pleasure and seeing if I can find a way to turn them on that they have never experienced before, the connecting.

As a relationship coach, I feel so sad when I read about sex being over in a few minutes and 'foreplay' being non-existent. Even a massage or a back tickle can be a nice way to start sex off. But even if you both/all are already turned on when you meet up, fucking is more than making a penis and/or vagina wetter via orgasm. Sex can be the best free fun available if you want to truly explore some of the possibilities of arousal within it.

Also, on those days where you want to be intimate but are really not in the mood for sex, for whatever reason, touch in the right way can be really validating. A mum who is feeling all touched out may feel really loved and valued through having her feet massaged. A tired and stressed person studying for exams, might love to just lay and cuddle and idly stroke their lover's hair and so on.

50

Sights

 *Lila - she/her, straight*

He likes to be able to see. To see his cock entering my pussy or my ass. He likes to position us in front of a mirror. I was shy initially but then I could see too and learnt why he found it such a turn on. Changing speed or depth and being able to see the whole body reaction as well as the wetness dripping out and around the tops of my legs or down the crack of my ass. Seeing it makes it more of a turn on.

The big window serves as a mirror at night, and I can see both under and over and around. We get different views of each other, of cock moving in and out. Of balls getting tighter and tighter ready to release.

He loves the sight of his handprint, red on my ass cheeks. Not yet aware that the sting will be more intense and erotic if he dips his fingers in my dripping pussy first. The wet fingers slapping in an impact that is different to dry fingers. His cum dripping out of me, onto the floor. What a beautiful sight.

Some people will only have sex in the dark, under the covers, not confident in the way their body looks or feels, or ashamed of sex. Some people are taught that sex is a duty or a right, but not that it is a gift or a pleasure to be enjoyed. Some people are focused on getting or not getting pregnant, others on transitioning to a body they are comfortable in.

If you are not comfortable in your own body, it is incredibly hard to be comfortable in that body naked, especially around others. And if you are not comfortable in yourself, how can you connect to someone else. How can you relax into sexual pleasure? If this speaks to your experience at the moment, seeking support can help. There are also some things that you can do to help yourself too.

You do not have to love your body to be comfortable in it. Don't stress about loving it! You do not have to be naked to have sex. You do not have to have the light on. You do you. But do it kindly, be kind to yourself. Be open to enjoyment. Say no to things you are not comfortable with and people who do not make you feel good about yourself.

Learn how your skin feels when you touch it, experiment with different types of touch on your skin. Where on your body does it feel nice? Wear clothes to do this if it is more comfortable for you. Where is off limits to touch, for you or for others? No one is allowed to touch certain small sections of my body due to prior injuries/trauma. I am very clear with each person I have sex with. You cannot touch me here. Here is ok, here is not.

Only a very few people have attempted to touch where I have asked them not to. Usually, they apologise immediately, just not being used to having that boundary in place. One asked why. I told him. Rape, sexual assault, strangulation. He treated me even more kindly than he already did after that. I was ok to answer that question, not everyone will be.

51

Sounds

**T***om - he/him, pansexual*

I heard him take his belt off but didn't hear it being left on the chair. Then he was behind me, close enough to touch and I could hear the leather being folded in two. The anticipation excited me. I stood still against the sink where I had been brushing my hair and dropped the hairbrush as I heard the first flick back of the wrist and leather.

That beautiful sound as the folded leather met my bum was followed by an intake of his breath and an internal thank you and please don't stop. This was new for him, but not for me. I had not asked him to do this. From spanking me which he loved, he knew to slowly build, and the sound became louder and sharper with each thwack. I could feel my wetness increase with the sounds of his breathing as well as the belt.

"Do you like it?" He asked. It amazes me sometimes that he cannot read my pleasure. The pleasure that I am so noisy with. Grunts and words and breath and body movements all conveying how much and what I want. I could hear my yes, split seconds before the belt's sharp thwack on a now red lined bottom and I knew his excitement was as great as mine.

The sound of him physically pulling my legs apart so he could get his cock in my wetness was almost unbearably pleasurable. I knew I would get both the punishment and the reward.

I have very hard limits on any kind of impact play; spanking, whips, paddles, crops, switches etc. Pink, red temporary marks are good, welts and bruises are not ok.

Impact play takes skill. It needs to be done in ways that do not do permanent damage to organs as illustrated earlier. It also needs to be within the safe, sane and consensual limits of all concerned.

As the endorphins (happy chemicals) get released during impact play, it can be hard to regulate the force to that safe, sane, consensual, pre-agreed level, which is why you should start with hands and not whips or paddles. You should also only engage in impact play with someone that you have already built a rapport with. Between the two of you, you need to be able to stick to those agreed limits and to stop immediately if either of you use your safe word,

Limits can be rediscussed between sessions. However, if the person doing the spanking, whipping, paddling etc noticing that the person receiving it is starting to 'space out', they should at the very least pause for a check in and unless you are experienced playing in this way with THIS person, you should stop. Agreed aftercare should be used to bring the person back into themselves and then you can discuss if you want to do anything else or not for the moment.

52

Porn

Porn is ubiquitous, freely available online and can be either a healthy addition to your sex life or it can destroy your finances, relationships and even sexual enjoyment if you become addicted to porn. Especially if you are addicted to porn that is not representative of reality and/or costs money and/or is illegal.

There is a really great organisation in Australia with two branches, one called Porn is Not the Norm (PINN) (https://www.not-thenorm.com.au/)and one called Its Time we Talked (https://it-stimewetalked.com/) that both have some wonderful information and useful resources on their website. I have been so shocked over the last ten years by how many people think that sex depictions within porn are accurate representations of sexual acts. They rarely are. In the last year or so, AI has become more and more common in all aspects of porn. As PINN (2024) state on their website; "Pornography has become a default sexuality educator, with serious implications for young people's capacity to develop a sexuality that is safe, respectful, mutual and consenting."

I see videos where the women have bodies that more closely resemble barbie dolls of old than real human beings. And yet somehow, people, mostly men, think this represents reality. The rise of stepparent-stepchild porn is concerning as it normalises interactions that are at best unethical and extremely mentally damaging and at worst illegal and contemptible.

Strangulation is depicted as pleasurable in porn so much that evidence suggests up to 75% of young adults engage in strangulation despite it not being pleasurable for most of the people being strangled. Worse, even if the person being choked or strangled does not die, there are cumulative brain damaging effects due to the restriction of oxygen to the brain during the strangulation period.

Even porn that uses actors or 'real people' has fake elements within it. BDSM scenes show no concerns for safety and safe sex is rarely depicted on any kind of porn. All these factors contribute to the wider community understanding of sex, relationships and the concepts of safe, sane and consensual.

53

Squirting

 *my - she/her, bisexual*
I cannot count how many times I have been asked if I am a squirter. However, it is only marginally more times that a sexual partner has been surprised that the sheets under us are wet after sex in bed. One type of sexual partner watches a lot of porn (the squirter questioner), and one is naïve and/or not very experienced as has no idea that bodily fluids follow the laws of gravity (the surprised person).

Squirting refers to liquid being expelled from a vagina during orgasm. It is important to note that only some people with vaginas squirt during orgasm, and even those who do squirt often only do so sometimes. This type of orgasm includes a rapid ejection of urine, along with other fluids, from the bladder. Most people who do squirt, cannot control when or how much they squirt during orgasm. Some of these people will experience multiple small squirts or they will squirt once before orgasm not during.

Squirting does not always mean there is a high-volume of liquid that soaks the sheets. Squirting ranges from a very tiny amount of liquid to a full-on stream of liquid. Porn usually shows a large stream of liquid, which is faked for dramatic effect. It is the porn equivalent of fake blood in a horror movie.

WebMD reports that; Researchers disagree on what the fluid released during squirting is. Some small studies have found that it comes from the bladder and has some urine in it. But in some cases, it can also have high levels of glucose and prostate-specific antigens (PSAs), which come from the Skene's glands. People who have experienced squirting also say that the fluid doesn't look, smell, or taste like urine. It's safe to say that it's similar to pee but not the same." (https://www.webmd.com/sex/what-is-squirting-orgasm , 2023)

If you or the person you are with do not squirt, this does not mean that they are not enjoying the sex or orgasm. It simply means that is not how that body works.

If you or the person you are having sex with do squirt or even just have a lot of bodily fluids dripping out during sex, waterproof sheets or blankets can be really helpful to have on the surface where you are having sex. These are often referred to as splash blankets, waterproof sex sheets or waterproof adult intimacy bedding.

Alternatively, you can use regular sheets with a waterproof mattress protector and just wash the sheets after sex. It is important to protect your mattress from getting wet with any bodily fluids, as this can stain the mattress but more importantly sink into it and cause mould etc to develop over time.

54

Deep throat

 It has become far more common for people to ask others if that can deep throat. Deep throating refers to when the person sucks the depth of the entire penis with their mouth. This is commonly represented as the norm in porn, starting in 1972 with a movie of the same name, but the reality is totally different.

Humans almost universally have a gag reflex that makes them gag or even vomit if anything hits a particular spot in their throat. This spot is always hit during deep throating. I love this line from Cosmopolitan magazine online; "Deep throating is super easy and comfortable if you're a professional sword swallower without a gag reflex." (https://www.cosmopolitan.com/sexopedia/a8273350/deep-throat-blow-job/)

I can totally understand that this feels amazing for men, but it can be awful for any person who is actually giving oral/head (blow job/BJ/oral), even those who love giving oral. The sensation is like choking, and for some people will result in instant vomiting.

If you chose to deep throat and it is something you enjoy, the saliva produced by the gagging acts as a lubricant. People who work in porn know that some deep throating is faked with camera angles and body doubles or AI etc and that where it is real, the actor, male or female, has spent time and energy perfecting the technique. Much in the same way as a sword swallower has spent the time and energy to perfect what is essentially the same technique.

Never use numbing spray during head as it can prevent the body from knowing when you need to stop. Whenever giving a BJ, it is much easier if the person who is doing the sucking is the one in control. However, this can feel daunting to say or do as porn almost always shows the person whose dick is being sucked controlling the other person's head. Usually with their hand on the back of their head, or by holding/pulling their hair. This is counterproductive and can lead to increased choking/gagging sensations or even avoidance of this act.

If you are giving head/oral to a person with a penis there are a number of things that make this easier for you and still just as or even more pleasurable for them:

- Wrap your hand around the base of their cock to control how much of the cock can actually enter your mouth
- Start off by licking up and down and around the cock which helps to lubricate it
- Be in control, it is totally ok to choose the position that works best for you. You can tell people that if they push their dick in too deep for you, that you will vomit on them, especially if this is the case!
- Check how far a foreskin, if there is one, is comfortable being moved
- Suck the cock very gently to more firmly, ask the person to let you know which is best, which they want the most of, at what point in their arousal, etc
- Use your tongue to lick the cock whilst sucking, this gives your jaw a break
- Use your tongue to lick around the head of the cock as it exits and enters your mouth

- If the person is circumcised there is often a small ridge at the back of the cock where the head joins the shaft. Flicking this with your tongue can be very pleasurable and provides time to breathe deeply without having your mouth full
- Alternate sucking as deeply as you are comfortable with moving your mouth and tongue up and down the cock

Please note it is also common to NOT want the person to cum/ejaculate in your mouth. If you do not like the taste of cum or have any other reason for not wanting this, either stop before they cum and/or make sure they KNOW beforehand that you are not ok with this.

The way you can word this is to explain that you like the taste of precum but will vomit if they cum in your mouth.

Anna - *she/her*

I was giving a boyfriend a BJ, we had been together a while at this stage, and they knew I wasn't comfortable with swallowing. However, they ejaculated before I realised they were going to and found out the hard way that I was not joking about vomiting. I also got incredibly angry with them as they had not asked before cumming. We had a massive argument, and they did apologise profusely and never did this again.

I am aware that he just got carried away and we had known each other for years at this point and it had never happened before. Mostly, the people I give BJs to ask me to stop, put a condom on and then we fuck, so that they cum inside me (inside the condom). A few ask me to stop and ask where on my body they can cum and then they masturbate until they cum on me.

It is good to have these conversations about preferences before you start any sexual activity, as a safe assumption is that without a conversation, enjoyment will be less for one or more of you.

55

Connecting

Jo - they/them, non-binary

The need is too deep. The ache too primal. The desire too overwhelming. Interesting how I weigh my needs, wants and desires against what society says is acceptable and what groups within deem necessary. Not an inch of masochism in me but almost equal amounts of dom and sub with an almost insatiable appetite for sexual pleasure.

Contrast that with the very human yearning to connect and to matter. Not necessarily to be the one and only person in someone's life, but to be an important person, whether just during playtime or outside of that.

And yet that does not mean I want to be anybody's. I want to feel a genuine spark, again whether that it is purely during play or outside of it. If there is no spark, there is no connection.

Age, gender, status, job, money etc, these are nothing. Kindness in life, caring in play (however that might look) and the ability to hold a conversation, these are the turn ons that get me really excited and interested.

I'm the kind of person that people share their life story with, whilst I am more reticent and need to be asked about myself. Not asking implies no con-

nection and no matter how great the other person may be, my interest flickers out.

Many people assume that someone who loves sex will be willing to have sex with anybody, but this is rarely the case, even for sex addicts. Most people have a human need to matter, to feel valued and valuable. Within poly or ENM relationships, being a secondary partner, still means that you matter and are valued by and valuable to your partner.

In hookup culture, hooking up or ONS are meant to be devoid of connection and value, to be NSA, no strings attached. This does not refer to literal strings, though ONS involving bondage are inherently risky unless you already know and trust the person. Having sex with someone can be purely physical and there is nothing wrong with that. But when a person years for connection, purely physical sex can leave them feeling empty and sad.

This may be one of the reasons for the rise of FWBs as a way to meet both physical sexual and emotional needs. If you like and have a friendship with the person you are fucking, then you have an emotional connection, you matter to each other.

56

Threesomes and more

Another very common theme in porn. One person being fucked or otherwise pleasured by two or more people, who are totally focused on that one person. Their orgasms being the sole point of the sex. In reality, threesomes and more are much more complicated, unless set up specifically for the orgasms of one, with the consent and agreement of all concerned.

In reality, many people are not going to be happy focusing solely on someone else, especially if one or more other people are also doing so! What about you and your pleasure?

Recently I decided to actually ask one of my cis male friends, who has been making it clear he wants a threesome for a while now, what he envisaged that would look like in reality. His response was that it would be two women focusing on his body and his pleasure. I was astounded. Did he really think that the two women would be content touching, kissing, licking, sucking and fucking just him and not interacting with each other at all?

When I asked him this, he, to his credit did think about it a little bit. Response was something along the lines of him not having really thought about that before. So, I wondered what his previous threesomes had been like, and if he was willing to share some information about how they were. He told me that he has had two or three of them, all with now ex-girlfriends and friends of theirs. None of the women involved were sexually attracted to women and so they were just focused on him.

Women who are attracted to other women and to men are highly unlikely to be willing to focus purely on the male. One of the women interviewed for this book talked about a disastrous threesome that she had with a FWB and his wife. She had been told that they both wanted to play, however when it happened it became very obvious that the wife was totally straight and not interested in touching or being touched in anyway by a woman. Awkward all around!

Threesomes can be the most problematic of numbers involved as one person invariably feels left out more than the others. As humans, we are emotional creatures and can project or assume things that may or may not be real. The practicalities of who is involved in threesomes/ moresomes need to planned ahead of time. Who involved will be sexually attracted to and comfortable sexually engaging with who and in what ways.

Some straight identifying Male Female (MF) couples will only play with other females, whilst others will only play with other males and yet others only with other MF couple.

Is the action shared by all, or is someone watching only? Is everyone aware and comfortable with who is hoping to do what with who? What has been agreed about safe sex and condom and dental dam use? Where are you planning to play? If it is at a hotel/motel, who is paying? Are you socialising first or going straight into it? Who is bringing condoms/lube etc? Who is paying for those? Is it an alcohol and drug free play or not? If not are there any specific limitations?

Anna - *she/her*

Don't get me wrong, I very much enjoy three-somes and moresomes in some contexts. But that is pure exhibitionism and greed for as many orgasms as possible on my behalf. I don't actually enjoy the looking for the third person, the negotiating and setting it up etc. Such a lot of hard work for a little bit of fun. I'd rather just go to events or play parties.

57

Anal

Anal sex has been a part of human sexuality since time immemorial. Both straight and gay sex. One was used partly as a way to avoid pregnancy but still engage in sex, particularly prior to the easy and cheap availability of condoms, and the other purely for pleasure. In porn, anal sex is often rough and deep. Condoms and lube are rarely seen in porn.

However, safety is vital in anal sex as unsafe anal sex can cause anything from temporary pain, through long lasting pain and damage to permanent pain and damage or even death.

Mindy - she/her, straight

As someone who has suffered, and believe me it was suffering, from an anal tear due to an accidental injury during anal sex by a generally very careful and safe lover, I can honestly say, lube, condoms and care in anal play is extremely important. This is because there is NO naturally occurring lubricant and bacteria naturally lives in and around the anus, even with food hygiene.

Anal Sex

Anal sex can be with either fingers, cock or toys. See below for toys and plug play. Anal sex can be extremely pleasurable for some people, whilst it is just a complete turn off for some people. No judgement either way. Just because I like or do not like something in life does not make that thing inherently right or wrong.

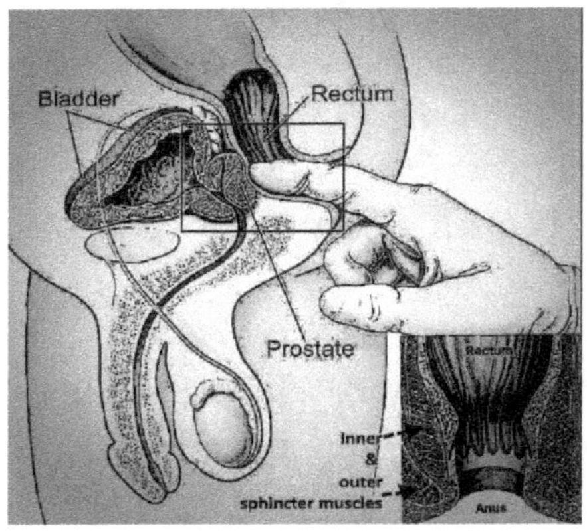

Alt text:
anatomical drawing of male genitals, bladder, rectum and prostate. Details of anus and anal sphincter ring muscles.

For this section, I am referring to anal sex as finger in anus or penis in anus. Anus owner is of any gender! If using fingers, make sure nails are cut short and filed so there are no sharp edges. Make sure your hands are clean, especially under the fingernails. You may choose to wear gloves, check re latex allergies as you can get non-latex gloves too.

The anus skin can be very fragile, more so for AFAB women than AMAB people.

1. Firstly, get explicit consent.
2. Secondly, apply lube.
3. Thirdly, get started.
4. Finally, check in that the person is enjoying throughout.

Be aware that small particles of poop may or may not end up on the finger/condom that is inside the anus. If you can't handle this don't do anal play.

When anything is first inserted into your anus, it can initially feel as if you need to poop. You don't but it can feel as if you do. Be gentle and make sure to use lots of lube.

Rub the lube around the anus and over your finger, or condom covered cock. If the person is new to anal sex, make sure to use a finger before trying to put your cock in their ass.

Rimming

Rimming is the kissing or licking of the outer edge (rim) of the anus. Rimming may also involve putting your tongue into the other person's anus. Rimming can be enjoyed by anyone, though some people will not be interested in trying it. Rimming can be very pleasurable because it stimulates the pudendal nerve, which in turn can turn people on. This nerve stimulates the penis and the vagina.

Remember with sex everyone needs to consent, if one person says no, then it's a NO.

There are health and sexual health risks with rimming, including possible contact with any bacterial or parasitic infections the person being rimmed may have as well as any sexually transmitted infections (STIs), which can also be spread through oral-anal contact. It is important to know that someone you would like to rim and who wants to be rimmed, is healthy and doesn't have any STIs. Hygiene is very important with rimming. To further reduce the risk of infections, you can use dental dams over the anus or any kind of glad/saran wrap.

Butt plugs/anal toys

If you are going to use anal toys, you should use ones that are specifically made for this. Because of the very delicate skin in the anus, it is easy to tear the skin which can cause both long-term pain and also infections etc. Anal tears sometimes heal on their own but can also need surgery or a Botox injection to enable the tissues to heal.

Butt plugs and anal toys come in a variety of shapes, sizes and materials. For beginners, silicon is much better than metal or glass. Silicon has is smooth and tends to match the body's temperature and have a little more flexibility/give than other materials.

Whatever you chose, needs to have a base so that it does not disappear up the colon. Anyone who has ever tried to retrieve a condom from inside the anal sphincter will know how hard that it. Retrieving toys or other objects tends to require medical assistance.

Sara - she/they, pansexual

The first time someone asked if they could put a butt plug in my ass whilst we played, I was curious but not entirely sure. I knew a finger felt good, but a finger is smaller than even the tiniest butt plug that I have ever seen. But I'm a sucker for shiny stuff. She showed me her butt plug, small and narrow with a shiny (fake) jewel in the base.

She asked me how cute I thought my ass would look with that nestled between by butt cheeks. It may well have looked cute,

I don't really know, but it felt soooo good. She tapped it with her open hand, so it just bounced a little in and out of my ass, until my pleasure built and built.

She said I couldn't cum until I begged her, in detail. "Please Mistress, may I cum from the butt plug in my ass as you spank my ass, and it pushes it and out of my ass." Satisfied with the detail and politeness of my request, she let me cum, praising me as her 'good girl', letting me know she would do this again.

As will all anal sex, toys and plugs need to be used with plenty of lube and need to be kept clean. Washing after and before play is a good idea. If anything causes a sharp pain, stop and gently remove the plug/toy.

58

Toys

Mia - *she/her*

When I first discovered just how much fun I could have with sex, it was much harder to buy toys than it is now. There was also much less choice than now. I went to an amazing sex shop in San Francisco which blew my mind. Local stores in the UK at that time, were downside streets with blacked out doors and windows and contained mainly clothes and toys for use in gay male sex.

To be fair, this may have been influenced by the company I kept, or my knowledge of what sex shops existed. However, now many high streets around the world have a sex shop. Where they don't there are online shops a plenty.

It can be daunting buying toys online for a variety of reasons, from not wanting the postie to know where you are shopping (they won't and even if they do, they don't care) to not realising exactly what you are buying. One of the first toys that I bought online was a lot bigger than I thought it was going to be judging from the highly inaccurate picture.

I have never used that toy, but I have learnt to actually read the descriptions.

If you are not sure how big that actually translates too, either measure an existing toy or your penis if you have one or put your fingers together and measure around the fingers. This can help you gauge both length and circumference.

Some people share toys and others don't. There is no right or wrong with this, as long as the toys are always kept clean and cleaned between uses.

There are toys for external use only such as swings and whips, and toys for internal use such as dildos and vibrators, often called vibes. Toys for penises, vaginas, anuses and non-specific toys. I have a small collection, about half of which I was left during various break-ups, as 'you will enjoy these more than I will going forward.'

If you currently don't get as much enjoyment from sex as you think is possible or as you would like, or sex is new to you, toys are a good way to explore what you like and don't like. With my first girlfriend, we really enjoyed each other's bodies, but she still wanted to explore dildos to complement our fingers and mouths. I had no issue with this, so we did.

Remote vibes are an interesting way to play with someone who you are not physically able to interact with. One or both of you insert a remote vibe, turn on the app, invite the other and give them the control of the vibe that is inside you. The apps enable remote control of not just the speed of the vibration, but also the pattern.

These vibes are inserted into the vagina usually, although some stimulate the clitoris as well or instead. They are often quite fiddly to charge up and can run out of charge over time, and not just when not being used.

As new ones are being released all the time, it is a good idea to read reviews before purchase. It is also a good idea to read around the apps and online communities before joining them.

Paula - *she/her, ENM*

I signed on to this discord group where randoms could control your remote vibe. I was feeling horny at the time and hadn't really looked into it properly and was totally shocked when I realised, we were audio connected. I hung up and deleted the group from my discord server immediately. From then on, I either played by myself or with a regular long distance partner.

Masturbation

All people, of any gender can masturbate. What that looks like will be individual. For intersex people, this may be more individual than for other people. Generally, masturbation is stimulating or playing with your own penis and balls or clitoris and vagina. Some people also engage in anal masturbation, with your fingers and/or with toys.

Masturbation is a good way to relax, release sexual tension and just generally have some pleasure. It is different to sexual activity with others, whether or not you use toys or just your own hands.

There are no health risks with giving yourself orgasms, as long as the toys or your hands are clean and used safely. It is not true that self-pleasure will lead to blindness or madness! It will however help you enjoy yourself and learn what kind of touch can bring you to orgasm.

Paula - *she/her, ENM*

Personally, I masturbate every night. It relaxes me so I can sleep well. It's not even always sexual, though it really is sometimes. If I get sent a long sext from one of my FWBs, I'll play with my clit whilst reading it, and then imagine what could happen next. I keep playing and imagining until I cum.

Other times it is literally just I can't sleep and if I play with myself in a certain way, I can get my entire body totally tense and then release and relax. Great way to fall asleep, if there isn't anyone around to actually have sex with. And then sometimes I use my remote vibe, if I'm not getting anyone else to control it then it's masturbation!

59

Orgasm control

Orgasm control is where the release of an orgasm is withheld for a period of time, or controlled as to when it can happen. Sometimes called edging, in orgasm control the idea is to heighten the pleasure and increase the intensity of the orgasm through building up to just before you/they cum and then stopping or changing what you do so the orgasm is denied. Then repeat until either they/you cannot stop the orgasm or until you/they want you/them to cum.

Recently I met someone new, who told me they were going to give me the best sex ever, through orgasm control. As an aside, it is highly inadvisable to say you are going to be the best ever as it is quite unlikely in 99.9% of cases, and it sets you up for failure. Just be and enjoy. Talking yourself up comes across as either insecurity or arrogance, neither of which are sexy or hot.

There are four main ways to play with orgasm control:

1. Chastity aides such as a cock cage or chastity belt. The wearer is unable to have sex unless they are let out of the cage/belt. There are a huge variety of these available, even on Amazon.
2. Remote vibe play. The person controlling the vibe gets to control the intensity of the vibe and so your orgasm.
3. Power play, the person being played with has to ask/beg to be allowed to cum. They may be denied repeatedly. Optionally,

they may be punished with a mutually agreed punishment if they cum without consent.

4. Power play, the person being played with has to ask NOT to be allowed to cum whenever they are close to cumming. They may do this by asking the person to stop or simply begging not to cum (yet). Again, mutually acceptable punishment may be given if the person cums without permission.

Simon - *he/him, straight, FWB, Dom*

I love playing with my sub, she is such a good slut. One of my favourite ways to play with her is to spread her legs wide open and restrain her in that position, either laying flat on the bed or standing up.

She cums so easily, that I love to make her beg me not to cum. When she begs not to cum, I stop whatever I am doing, licking her clit or pussy, fingering her pussy or ass or fucking her. And then I spank her, depending on what I have the easiest access to I will spank her ass or her clit. She can cum from either of these too, so sometimes I will spank until she begs me not to cum and then go back to what I had been doing before...

Her absolute pleasure and focus on her pleasure is so hot to see and hear and feel. She gets so wet, and when I finally do let her cum, I will keep going so she cums over and over, hard. When we play like this the spanking is a reward for being a good girl and not cumming, so she also needs to say thank you for each spank.

It is amazing how wet she can get from me telling her she is a good girl, and how much wetter from a quick spank on her clit. I know the first time we played like this, she was a bit worried it might hurt, and she is NOT into pain at all. But the clit spanks are not hard, they are just a different way of touching the clit and pussy all at the same time. If I spank just right my fingertips can dip into her dripping wet pussy when my palm makes contact with her clit.

However, if one person really struggles to orgasm, playing with orgasm control can be incredibly frustrating and unhelpful for the relationship. In this case, it can be helpful to spend some time focusing on other aspects of intimacy. This is sometimes described as; taking orgasms out of the equation. All people can sometimes struggle to cum, for some men it is difficult to get or to stay hard which impacts their ability to cum. Whereas some women just can't cum from penis in vagina sex or from any sex with others.

If sex is painful for one or more of the people, again orgasm control is not a good idea! Please see a Dr or sex therapist if sex is painful or you have some erectile dysfunction (ED) as most pain and ED can be treated fairly easily.

60

Period sex

Having sex during menstruation is a one no, then it doesn't happen or a two/all yes and its fine. Period sex is messier, even with condom or glove use. So, putting a towel down or having waterproof sheets is useful.

If period sex grosses you out, then don't do it, but don't be mean or unkind about it. Just say it is not for you.

If you are both cool to try it and haven't before, it should decrease period pain and not add to it. For many people, having an orgasm during their period is one of the best forms of pain relief. But for others their fear of grossing out the person they are with means it is all just anxiety provoking. So, as with any other kind of sex, communication is key.

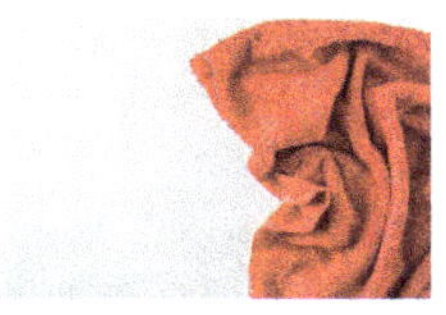

Sarah – lesbian, monogamous
I had this girlfriend who had a similar sex drive to me, so we usually had
sex once or twice a day. Before her, I had never had period sex, but she was

German and Germans seem a lot more comfortable with bodies and bodily processes than a lot of other cultures.

I remember kinda just saying that I was on my period as her hands were wandering into my pants. She said she didn't care and to just take my tampon out and she'd put a towel down for us to lay on. I always had such painful periods and that first period sex orgasm was just so intense and my cramps didn't bother me for a few hours after.

The towel was pretty messy after, but as my girlfriend said, so what. Rinsed it in the sink, then chucked it in the washing machine. That towel got a lot of use in that relationship!

61

Foot fetish

There are as many fetishes as you could imagine, and a fairly common one is a foot fetish. The Oxford English dictionary online defines a fetish as: "a form of sexual desire in which gratification is strongly linked to a particular object or activity or a part of the body other than the sexual organs."

So, for example, a person with a foot fetish means the person sexually desires feet or can only get sexual pleasure or gratification from some kind of interaction (looking may be enough) with feet.

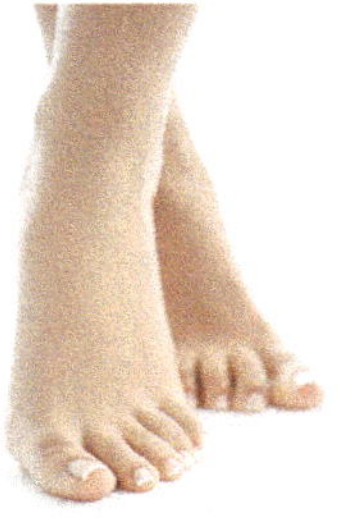

Wikipedia notes that Foot fetishism, also known as or podophilia (love of feet), is the most common form of sexual fetishism for otherwise non-sexual objects or body parts. https://en.wikipedia.org/wiki/Foot_fetishism As with most types of sexual desire, exactly what a podophilia is attracted to is quite individual.

It may be toenails, the ankle, the toes or the whole foot. What bring the sexual gratification can be looking, touching or integrating into sex, by for example using the feet to stroke the penis or pussy. It may be kneeling at the feet of a person wearing high heels and licking their shoes. It may be something else entirely.

There is nothing inherently wrong with a fetish that is carried out safely and consensually and is not breaking any laws. With any fetish, it is important to be open and have honest discussions about your desires and pleasures as it is never ok to involved anyone in your fetishes without their consent.

62

Conversations about sex

All new sexual play partners or relationships should have conversations about sex. This is much more comfortable for some people than others. These conversations can start as gently or explicitly as the people within them are comfortable with. If you are not sure, perhaps err on the side of caution and be less explicit that you would be if you knew the other person really well.

If the conversation is online rather than in person it can seem like its ok to start really explicit. However, if you do that you run the risk of being blocked immediately by the other person, if that was not what they were both looking for and expecting.

For example, in setting up some play sessions with a friend, T made some Kik groups to transfer the chat to once they had done an initial check on another site/app. T came into one group chat on what looked like the second exchange, as the guy asked if they both liked anal... T private messaged that she felt that was a bit forward and her friend replied explaining that sex had already been brought up in the last half and hour of chats, so it was at that stage for them.

Many people are happy to have an explicit conversation after the initial; what are you looking for, where are you based, how old are you, are you single or poly or ENM or open relationship. T likes to get to know people a bit better first. Neither is wrong, neither is better than the other, everyone is just different.

T said: "Sorry Jess! I'll be more reflective and inclusive next time. It is probably because I am usually aiming to meet other BDSM people to play with and those conversations often start with; what are your likes, dislikes and hard no's?"

Personally, when dating or looking to meet people, I will usually delete and block if a conversation is started with a crotch shot (of any gender), no matter how 'impressive' the picture is. Whereas some people are fine with this, it is more that case that most people who do not do this are NOT fine with it. Torso pics or fully clothed pics are the most appropriate pics to send.

For safety reasons, many people will not disclose exactly where they live nor what they do for work. It is helpful therefore to chat in ways that support that safety. Instead of asking where they live, ask what side of town they live on, or what city they live in or near. Ask what kind of industry they work in, if they are employed, or what subject they are studying, if they are studying.

Be honest about how old you are. You might say I am in my 40s rather than, I am 48, which is fine. But saying you are 38 when you are 45 is not ok. If you lie, then if a relationship develops, you have at some point, got to own up to and undo the lie. Also be honest about what you are looking for and what your relationship status(es) are currently.

Mia - *she/her, ENM, pansexual*
I have only had one vicious response to my honesty, which was some guy who had already disclosed he had been single for years and struggled to get a second date.

He told me I would die alone and lonely and was basically a terrible excuse for a human being. I think it was a case of him being unkind and sour bitter and twisted about his dating experiences rather than an indictment on the way I choose to live my life.

The conversation – dating

At some point after meeting online or in real life and spending time together over a period of days or weeks or months, someone is going to want to have the conversation. This conversation aims to clarify the early stage of the relationship. Are the two/more of you dating? Is that dating exclusive or not? At this point, some couples/thruples etc will find out they are incompatible, as for example, one person may desire ENM/poly/open whilst the other person wants an exclusive monogamous relationship.

Without this conversation taking place, the default expectation is usually that the people involved *may* be seeing or even having sex with other people. However, sometimes one or more of the people thinks that the default is exclusive dating. Where this is the case, people can end up in very confusing situationships where they really have no idea if the person is even interested in them at all or is only using them to have sex every so often. Even if you have the conversation, it is good to check in that you are both/all on the same page.

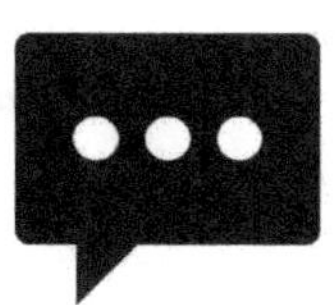

Mia - *she/her, ENM, pansexual*

When breaking up with a boyfriend once, it became apparent that even though I told him I have FWBs and was ENM that he thought once we were in a relationship, that it was monogamous, particularly because he did not have another sexual partner.

In contrast, I lived with someone for a number of years who veered wildly between saying we were in an open relationship to saying they were single and we were FWBs. Even though we were having sex daily. This was a par-

ticularly messy situation and a good example of a situationship. I put up with it because like most people in these messy situationships, I thought that love was enough.

Love is never enough. Respect and kindness are also needed and indeed vital.

ENM/Poly/Open relationships Conversations

Where people chose not to be monogamous, usually they will also decide how they want to structure their sexual intimacy and relationships/play partners. Most structures are framed with rules about what is and is not ok either for each individual or the couple/thruple etc.

For example, James and Louise were in a relationship. When they met James identified as bisexual and ENM and Louise as pansexual and Poly. For James, his personal rules were; deep love and connection only for his primary partner. He could have unlimited partners of any gender as long as everyone was having safe sex and everyone knew he was ENM. For Louise, her personal rules were that she could have deep love and connection with several people, but that all those people's sexual partners needed to be comfortable with her being with their partner. She was open to living with a primary partner.

Once James and Louise decided they wanted to be in a long term relationship, they sat down to negotiate the rules around their open ENM/poly relationship. They agreed that James could continue to have as many one night stands or FWBs as he wanted, as long as he only slept the night at home. They agreed that Louise could be in poly relationships, as long as she only slept the night at home. Both Louise and James, had a rule that all potential and current (play) partners needed to know that they were primary partners in a committed relationship.

This worked well for a few years until James asked Louise to choose between himself and the woman that Louise had been seeing for about six months on a regular basis. James did have some regular FWBs, but he wasn't deeply attached or connected to them and felt that he was becoming jealous of the love and care Louise had for her secondary partner. Even though both people were following their rules, things had emotionally shifted for James over the years, and he became monogamous following their breakup.

Louise continued to be poly for a while and then became ENM because she struggled to find others in the poly community to be in authentic relationships with. It is important to be honest with yourself and others about where you are at emotionally and in terms of managing your emotions about others.

Jealousy can be worked through if everyone wants to work through it and continue the relationship(s). But if the commitment to work through it and manage it isn't there, then jealousy destroys relationships. Jealousy is sometimes around attachments, real or perceived and sometimes it is about the amount of time that each person is getting.

James and Louise had a date night once a week initially, but over time that date night was replaced with just being home together. This was enough for Louise, but James struggled with his jealousy around Louise's girlfriend having dates several nights a week. He felt this meant that Louise was prioritising her girlfriend over him.

In reality, as a couple James and Louise had very little spare money to go on dates that cost anything. Whereas Louise's girlfriend had spare money and liked to go out for dinner after work and then have sex before Louise went home. James' FWBs were all people he just hung out with and then fucked with. All these little details are the things that non-monogamous relationships can get caught up on and fail over. Especially if they are not openly discussed and worked on to find a mutually acceptable solution.

Conversations need to cover rules about:

- Whether sex with others is individual, only as a couple or both
- If permission is needed before having sex with others or not
- If saying that you are going to have sex with someone else is necessary and if that should be before or after the sex
- Who is and is not allowed in terms of other sexual partners, e.g. friends, exes etc
- Acceptable frequency of play with others versus together
- Any sexual or emotional intimacy that is out of bounds
- Exactly what safe sex practices are required, e.g. are dental dams/condoms required for oral or not
- Where play with others can and cannot take place
- When play with others can and cannot take place
- How open you are going to be about the type of relationship you are in
- If others need to know you have other partners or not

If you cannot find mutually acceptable answers to all of these questions, then being non-monogamous is not going to work for you with that person. You then have a choice, to break up or continue to find a way to make things work for you BOTH/all.

63

BDSM

BDSM relationships can be open or monogamous. They are usually set up far more explicitly than other kinds of relationships or play sessions. Generic consent and explicit non-consent are all discussed before anything sexual takes place (or it should be and if it isn't then you are NOT ready for a BDSM relationship).

As a minimum, if you are going to play or be in a relationship with defined roles such as Dom/Sub etc, then these need to be explicitly defined and agreed. In addition, no play/sex should take place without having agreed what play is and is not acceptable, hard no's, aftercare and what each person's safe word is.

Everyone should have a safe word to minimise potential disasters. It is always ok to use a safe word and then sex/play must stop immediately and agreed aftercare implemented. Aftercare serves to ground everyone back into everyday reality and varies between people. My preferred aftercare is cuddles with one hand flat on my back and my head nestled into their chest/shoulder. I am happy to provide other aftercare, but if receiving that is what grounds me.

If impact play or restraints are being used, explicit conversations need to take place about any medical or psychological issues that need to be taken into account, as well as clear limits and boundaries. One of the reasons to discuss these first is that BDSM activities can release lots of endorphins (happy chemicals in the brain) which can make it hard it make good decisions during play.

Pippa *- she/her, lesbian, monogamous*

I have been into BDSM since I was 17, when my first girlfriend introduced me to it. She liked to tie me up and touch and finger fuck me until I was unable to stop continuously orgasming. At that point, nothing in the world exists for my but my body and the sensations it is experiencing. We had such an amazing relationship, but it sadly ended when we both moved to opposite sides of the country to study.

Unfortunately, when I was at university, I got involved with a new woman. I did not realise until it was way too late, that she was a narcissist and all the nice stuff at the beginning was her love bombing me. It turns out that yes, lesbians can be violent and aggressive to their partners too.

Anyway, she would just ignore my safe word and do stuff to me that I didn't want when she felt like it. I now know that I should have broken up with her the first time she did that, but I was honestly just in shock that a woman could physically hurt me. Even though she would claim it was just part of the BDSM play, it wasn't because it was not consensual. Safe, sane and consensual is a refrain in the BDSM world for a reason.

64

Fetishes

As mentioned in the foot fetish section, it is important to communicate properly about fetishes. There can be a lot of stigma and shame around some fetishes, so it can feel difficult to broach the topic. It can help to go into the conversation with two basic premises that:

1. Sharing what your fetish is with someone is not committed anyone to engaging in that fetish
2. Someone that treats you unkindly for being open and vulnerable is not worthy of your time and energy.

Bear in mind that not wanting to engage in your fetish with you is not being unkind. Trying to coerce or otherwise force someone to try your fetish is unkind and unhealthy. Coercion should never be a part of a healthy sexual relationship.

It is helpful to have conversations about fetishes, especially if you are unsure that the other person/people share your desires, when you are not in the middle of sex. Be calm and explain that you want to talk about some of your sexual desires that you haven't yet shared. Or if you think your partner has a fetish that you want to confirm or otherwise, just calmly ask them if they are ok to talk about sexual desires that you have been wondering if they have.

Try to be open and honest, without judging yourself or the other person. Sometimes, what comes up is totally new, so there may be lots of questions. It can be helpful to be encouraging of questions as the more shared knowledge there is the less that fear of the unknown can rear its ugly head!

It is nice to thank the person for listening/sharing and to be up-front about whether not being able to engage in the fetish is a deal breaker or not, but that you respect their decision.

Using consent cards at this point can be helpful so that the other person can express their interest level without needing to explicitly engage. A great example of these cards can be found at:

https://www.printerstudio.com/sell/designs/50-shades.html

https://www.printerstudio.com/sell/designs/connect-ignite-your-passion-have-fun.html

Sometimes it is much easier to interact using these kinds of cards than it is to say what you are interested in. This is just due to societal conditioning. Again, as long as your fetish is legal and doesn't harm anyone, then there really isn't any shame in it.

65

Talking about Porn

There are two main conversations to be had around porn:

1. Do you watch porn/mind it I watch it?
2. I think you have a porn addiction which is impacting our sex life.

The first conversation is clearly less fraught than the second but can be relationship ending if the people are on totally different pages about porn. Especially in relation to porn that is paid for, such as OnlyFans or porn subscriptions.

Some people are comfortable with watching or reading free porn but not with paid porn, whilst for others it is the type of content that makes it ok or not ok. Porn that depicts illegal sexual activity or violence is less likely to be seen as ok by many people, but others say it is only acting and so its fine.

Because people's attitudes to porn can be quite complex it is important to ensure that your conversation ends up with a shared understanding of the porn parameters within your relationship.

- Is any porn ok to watch? Alone? Together?
- Is there some porn that is not ok to watch together?

- What about watching porn alone? Is there any porn that the other person would consider cheating?
- How frequently is it ok to watch porn? Alone? Together?
- Is it ok to masturbate to porn?
- What about having sex with porn on at the same time?
- What about OnlyFans? Subscription services?

Because each person has an individual perspective, you need to work through all possible areas of future conflict. Social media is full of people breaking up because of a perception of cheating when porn is involved. And I am not going to judge anyone for their personal ethics, morals and values around the myriad of pornography available.

If your partner has vastly different religious and political views to you, you may feel quite differently about porn.

Sam *- he/him, bisexual, open relationship*

I grew up really religious and hadn't really heard of or seen porn until I moved to America. And wow, what an experience, all these different ways of viewing sex and bodies. All day and night. For other people in my community, porn is seen as really taboo, like you would never ask your wife if she wants to watch it.

I have a FWB from outside the community and she will watch porn with me sometimes, but I don't know that she actually enjoys it much. When I asked her about it, she said she knows it can turn me on, but she would rather play with me or read porn if she doesn't have a physical person there to play with.

She will happily however, act out some stuff that I have watched and want to try out. If she isn't into it, she just says that isn't for her, what else would I like to try. It's great. I have learnt so much about what is actually real and possible and what is make believe. Some porn is so fake, no-one can actually do that!

The porn addiction conversation is much harder. Because, in all likelihood it is only needing to happen because the sexual side of your relationship is not going well. It is helpful to use I statements in this kind of conversation, instead of you statements.

You can alternatively start off by asking if they are satisfied with your sex life, or if there is anything they would like to improve. Let them know what you have noticed has changed in the last x amount of time. For example, "I have noticed that we don't seem to be having sex as much as we did three months ago. I really liked the way you caress my back when you want sex, and I realised I am missing that. Is there something that we need to work on?"

Or you can get straight to the chase; "You don't seem to be interested in sex with me anymore. I noticed you are watching a lot of porn. Do you think the porn is impacting your desire for me?"

66

Talking about Toys

Some people enjoy using sex toys for solo play to aide masturbation, and some don't. Some people like to include the use of sex toys in their intimate interactions with others, and some don't. There is no generic right or wrong, rather just a what feels right for you, individually or collectively, in the moment.

Before introducing your sex toys to someone else it can be helpful to have an introductory conversation to gauge attitudes. Interestingly, some people take their favourite sex toys to hook ups, especially if they are wanting an ongoing/ repeat session with the other person.

Simon – he/him, straight cis het male – FWBs
When I meet a new potential FWB online, we chat for a few months before we meet. During covid, that upped to 6-12 months. During this chatting period, I use the time to ensure we are on the same page about sex, what kinds of things we each find enjoyable, both receiving and giving.
We do talk about other stuff too, but it's mainly sex. I always ask about toys as when I fuck, I like to have a butt plug in me, and if my FWB is also into butt plugs, to use one on them too. I travel to FWB hook ups with my butt plug already in place. Gets me really horny and ready to fuck. I also like to slip a cock ring on once we are both clearly ready to fuck. If my FWB doesn't

have her own butt plug, I have a second one that I will bring with me. Obviously, I keep them clean, disinfecting both after use, and just before use.

__Dr Mattel__ – he/him, ENM: I love toys, I collect them. I review them and modify their use if required. When a woman comes to play with me, she can see some of my toys. The ones I'm going to use to play with her. They will be all laid out on the table in front of the play space where she will be able to take in the coming possibilities. Different toys have different effects on different people. Play should always be safe, sane and consensual, which means not only is hygiene important, but that people can withdraw their consent at any time. What feels good on one day, may not feel good another time, or the sensation may just get too intense, and the person may want a break or a time out.

67

Neurodivergent dating/ relationships/ sex

When I started writing this book, I was asked by a number of people, both neurodivergent and not, to include a section on the impact of neurodiversity on dating/relationships/sex. Neurodiversity is the concept that every human has a unique brain, that there is neurodiversity amongst the population.

Neurodivergent (ND) people are those whose brains are atypical to the majority of people, who can be viewed as neurotypical (NT). So autistic people, those with ADHD, those who are AuDHD as well as those with mental health conditions, including anxiety and depression are all neurodivergent.

The thing about neurodivergence is that it is highly individualised and personal in impact and presentation. But, basically ND individuals perceive, interpret and respond to the world around them in unique ways. This can impact dating/relationships and sex in various ways, due to two main areas; sensory differences and communication differences.

Sensory

We have 8 well understood senses, most of which are used when interacting with others and during intimacy and sex.

- Sight
- Hearing
- Oral/taste
- Touch
- Smell
- Balance/vestibular
- Sense of body in space/proprioception
- Sense of internal body signals/interoception

Sight

Visual input can be pleasurable, distracting and/or painful for ND individuals. This means that lighting may cause issues as might particular patterns or colours on bedding, flooring or other objects in the space.

Many ND people struggle with bright lights preferring dim lights and preferring LED lights over fluorescent lighting. Natural light may be problematic if the sun is particularly bright and shining directly into the space.

Some visual input that is pleasurable or fascinating to the ND person may add to the sexual enjoyment for everyone or distract the other person.

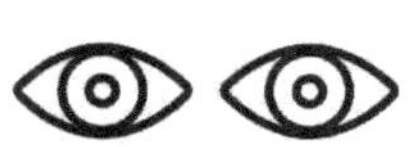

__May__ - AuDHD: When I was a teenager and first discovered penises I was fascinated with how they looked, and how the shape and texture changed when I touched them. I would spend ten to fifteen minutes at a time just staring at and playing with my boyfriend's penis.

I am not sure that he found this as fun as I did. If he had known I was AuDHD I think he would have understood a bit better that this was really a visual stim for me.

Hearing

Many ND individuals have some sensory sensitivity around sound. Again different sounds can be fascinating and/or painful and/or pleasurable or neutral. Where a person struggles with particular sounds, hearing these can negatively impact mood and desire. In contrast, where a particular sound is pleasurable the person can be really focused on creating or making that sounds.

__Leroy__ – autistic: I really love hearing the squelch of a wet pussy as I am fucking. It is such a big turn on for me, brings me sensory joy as well as sexual joy. I know that the woman being really wet will lead to this sound, so I make sure to get her really aroused with touch and kissing etc before I start to fuck her. This way, nearly every time we have sex, I will get to hear this sound. My girlfriend knows that I love this sound and she is happy that I enjoy it so much.

Oral/taste and smell

Tastes during sex can be perceived of with disgust or joy or neutral. When something is interpreted as tasting disgusting by a ND individual they will avoid that taste at all times. This needs to be respected as having to taste that taste will be traumatic as is likely to result in vomiting as in the earlier story where Anna's boyfriend came in her mouth without permission.

Jack – *ND: I hate the smell and taste of a women's pussy. Disgusting, doesn't matter how clean it is I just can't taste it. I prefer to have sex in ways that keep her pussy as far away as possible and in positions that mean I will get the least amount of her wetness on me or my condom.*

This doesn't mean I hate straight sex, I like it. It just means it needs to be done how I like it.

Touch

ND individuals can have more significant and atypical reactions to touch than other people. Light touch may be perceived of as painful and firm touch pleasurable or vice versa or any number of other interpretations. If you are or have an ND intimate partner it is really important to understand what touch is pleasant and what touch is horrible PRIOR to having sex.

The three minute game at the end of this book can be played as a 5 or 10 second game with a partner or you can experiment alone.

***Lila** – AuDHD: I love touch, I mean I love to be touched and to touch. A person's fingers on my skin is my happy place. Sex is definitely a sensory stim* *for me. It really brings me so much joy. So do back tickles and a hand gently stroking me all over. Ecstasy. Not everyone understands this though and I know I have had an autistic partner who hated being tickled, it would make him really upset and angry. He needed minimal firm touches and then it was penis in vagina until he came, then we were done. Needless to say, we were not exactly sexually compatible and that relationship ended quite quickly.*

Balance/vestibular

Our sense of balance is governed by our inner ear and most people don't really think about balance in a sexual context, however, many sexual positions require more balance from one of the people involved, than the other.

If someone has a very poor sense of balance they may need to be in particular positions or avoid unsupported standing sex.

Sense of body in space/proprioception

Our sense of our body in space is how we know where our body ends and space, objects or others begin. All people who appear clumsy, are in fact just struggling with their proprioception. In a sexual setting this can look like someone being uncoordinated and/or banging into people and things etc.

Sense of internal body signals/interoception

Our interoception signals body sensations as well as states of being and our emotions. Many ND people have better interoception in some areas than others, whilst some have minimal or no interoception in all areas.

Interoception impacts how someone experiences attraction and intimacy as well as emotions as feelings. If someone doesn't have good interoceptive awareness they won't notice what they are feeling and so it can be hard for them to know if they are or not enjoying intimate acts.

Another significant impact of poor interoception is difficulty understanding and expressing your own emotions. This can result in people seeming to fine even though they are getting really overwhelmed. When they are totally overwhelmed they go into their default survival mode; fawn, freeze, flop/drop, fight or flight. An unaware partner might think that a one off touch or comment has caused the overwhelm, when really it was a range of things leading up to that moment.

When learning about what intimacy you or a partner enjoy, if you/they have poor interoception, take things slowly and assume that any level of uncomfortableness is dislike. Feelings, if noticed, may only be noticed when they are very intense.

This may explain why some ND people really enjoy the intense feelings that go with BDSM.

Neurodivergent Communication

Neurodivergent (ND) people can be more literal with their language understanding than other people. It is important to say what you mean and mean what you say in both written and spoken language. Conversations may need to be more explicit than with non-

ND people, especially in the context of sex and relationships. ND individuals may not ask for clarity until they feel really comfortable or safe with someone.

Saying, be good to catch up next week is not clear enough for most ND people. Instead, it is more helpful to say when you can meet and how long for and what you would like to do. Asking what someone likes, is not specific enough. Asking if this touch feels good or not is.

ND people can have a blunt or to the point communication style, which can be mistaken for rudeness, but rarely is. They can also struggle to communicate when stressed, distressed or overwhelmed, with some ND people losing their regular ability to use speech to communicate.

ND individuals who do not use speech to communicate will often have an alterative communication system that can be high tech or low tech. Some ND individuals will prefer to have emotional or otherwise difficult conversations via text or email rather than with speech. Others find it easier to open up when doing an activity they love or when sitting next to rather than opposite.

Arguing can cause overwhelm for some ND individuals who may need space and quiet time to cam down, or they may need to seek out sensory input of their preferred kind.

68

Bodies

Bodies come in all different sizes, shapes, colours and abilities. For some people a person's body or their physical appearance is vey important and attraction is based on looks, whereas for others looks can be irrelevant. Some groups of people struggle more with dating than others due to preconceived notions or assumptions about their bodies. People who look different to the dominant culture within any context can be either seen 'exotic and highly desirable' or 'less beautiful/less desirable' by others. Ultimately there is no physical attribute that is universally desired and people will like what they like.

It is always ok to find someone attractive or not, it is how you handle this that matters. Be respectful and polite both when rejecting someone because they are 'not your type' and when flirting or trying to pick up or compliment someone.

Size/shape

Different body sizes and shapes can appeal to different people. Some people are attracted to slim people whilst others are attracted to those with curves or muscles etc. Body size can impact sex if the difference in size between the people involved is significant or if one of the people is clinically obese and unable to move around or reach their own genitals.

If someone is unhappy or uncomfortable in their own body, due to the way they view their whole or parts of their body, this can also impact intimacy. If you don't feel comfortable in your body then it can be hard to be at ease with sexual intimacy. Learning how your body can give you pleasure can help you to feel more comfortable being naked on your own or with someone else/others.

If someone is constantly criticising your body size or shape, or telling you that you need to lose weight for example, or they will not be attracted to you any more, that person is the problem not you. People are entitled to their own opinions and to find different things attractive or not. People are not entitled to trash someone's self esteem and confidence in pursuit of their ideal body type on someone else.

Be aware that cis gendered woman and people taking oestrogen can fluctuate in weight over the normal course of a month, anywhere from a couple to 10kg. Flying can also impact weight and people with food intolerance or gastrointestinal issues can experience bloating and/or weight fluctuations daily.

Pregnancy weight gain is healthy and can be very hard to lose for some people. Focus should be on health and wellbeing, post-partum and not weight!

Eating disorders are not gender specific and can be experienced by anyone. These are serious conditions, which can lead to significant health difficulties and even death in the wort cases. It is important to support those you love with help seeking if they are eating disordered.

Being honest and complimentary can bring a lot of happiness and confidence to some people. It is much easier to be sexually attracted to someone who says what they find sexy or beautiful about you, than it is if they do not give you compliments.

Pippa - she/her, cis female

I hadn't realised what a negative impact my ex had on my self-esteem and sexual self-confidence until I started dating again and this guy kept telling me how beautiful I was. I even rang up a friend to see if the new guy was love bombing me and him being complimentary was a red flag.

My ex never ever said anything complimentary to me, about anything. Considering he chose to be in a relationship with me, there had to be something he liked about me. To this day I have no idea what it was. I knew it wasn't the best relationship and I knew I wasn't sharing my authentic sexual self with him as I was quieter and more contained during sex with him that with anyone else I have ever been with. The absolute joy to be with someone who clearly relishes and ravishes my body and my mind it such a contrast.

Differently abled

People with bodies that are different or who use aides to move around, such as a wheelchair or walker can sometimes be perceived of as non-sexual. Just like the rest of the population, some will be asexual, and many will not. Society has often portrayed individuals with 'dis' abilities of any kind as infantile, unable to provide consent, not adult.

Whilst this may be true for some adults, it is untrue for others. Even individuals with intellectual disability have a right to express their sexuality in safe, sane, consensual manner.

If you have a body that is different from the typical, you may need to educate your sexual partners about the way you experience pleasure. What is and is not possible, how you need to be positioned or to position yourself for comfort and safety as well as pleasure.

If you are not yet sure about how you can experience pleasure, it is a good idea to explore your own body to see what feels good. If you are unable to touch yourself, you may want to explore in a more structured way with a sexual partner.

The three minute game, which can be changed to any time frame from 10 seconds to 3 minutes may be really useful in this scenario. See the 3 Minute Game chapter.

If you meet someone who is differently abled and are interested in intimacy with them, do not be afraid to ask respectful questions about how you can maximise their pleasure. You may want to ask about supports they may need to undress or transfer from a chair to bed or other surface for example.

Circumcised/cut vs uncut penis

Some people have preferences around a penis being circumcised or not. The visual look and the feel in a mouth or hand of a cut versus uncut penis is different. Having a preference is valid, being rude about the look or feel of someone's penis is not ok.

Hygiene practices for a penis can vary slightly between uncut and cut, with circumcision having origins in a perception that it was more hygienic. It's important to clean your penis daily with warm water. If you use soap, opt for a gentle, low irritant formula designed for sensitive skin. Avoid products like colognes, deodorants, body washes, lotions, or moisturizers that contain alcohol or perfumes.

If you have a foreskin, keeping it clean is crucial to prevent inflammation or infection. When washing, gently retract the foreskin and rinse the head of the penis and the area beneath the foreskin. Avoid forcefully pulling back the foreskin, as this can cause injury and potential scarring, leading to complications.

After washing the entire penis and scrotum (balls), gently dry the head of the penis with a towel. If you have a foreskin retract again, pat the area under it dry, and then return it to its normal position.

Please note that smegma is a natural buildup of dead skin cells and oily secretions which may accumulate under the foreskin in uncircumcised men. Regular cleaning is important to prevent excess buildup, which can cause odour and difficulty retracting the foreskin.

Avoid harsh scrubbing or forcing the foreskin back if smegma has hardened, as this can tear the skin and lead to infections. Clean the base of the penis and scrotum regularly and consider performing a Testicular Self Examination (TSE) each time.

All individuals, those with and those without a penis should change underwear at least daily, but also after exercising. Genitals of all kinds should be cleaned thoroughly after sexual activity to maintain hygiene.

Unusual symptoms such as itchiness, pain, tenderness, discharge, or rash around the head of your penis, could indicate balanitis, a common infection due to poor foreskin hygiene. Phimosis, another issue stemming from inadequate hygiene, can cause foreskin constriction. If you notice any changes in your penis, scrotum, or testicles, it's advisable to seek medical attention promptly.

People can worry about the size of their penis with an assumption being that bigger is better. However, this is not the case. A more reasonable assumption, based in truth, is that it is not the size it is what you do with it.

A penis can be used for rough or gentle intercourse/penetration of a vagina or anus as well as being given oral by someone. The speed and depth of penetration can vary and the pleasure experienced by both depends on this as well as other factors.

Size is both girth (width) and length. Both length and girth can mean that penetration can be painful if not worked up to with lots and lots of foreplay and often lots of lubricant/lube. Some people feel their penis is too small to pleasure someone else. This is rarely the case, but it can mean that the pleasure does not result in an orgasm for the other person.

With oral sex involving a penis, it is often more comfortable for the person whose mouth is around the penis, to be controlling the depth and movement. Most people's gag reflex is activated if the penis hits the back of their throat. For some people this can make them vomit. Porn depictions of deep throating are not accurate for the vast majority of people.

In addition, it is important to be considerate to the person giving you oral. Some people like the taste of both pre-cum and cu, whilst others like one but not the other and some do not like either.

Before cumming in someone's mouth consent should always be sought. This may look different for people in BDSM play, where consent may be given prior to any play taking place. For all other play/sex, consent should be asked for prior to ejaculation. Asking; 'where would you like me to cum' is much more likely to result in an answer that is genuinely consenting. Asking if you can cum in their mouth can create a sense of coercion for some people and result in them being less likely to want to suck and lick and kiss your dick in future!

Penetrating someone with a penis does not mean that the other person is guaranteed to orgasm from that penetration. Sex is so much more than penetration. Pleasure can come from so much more than just that one act. Some people like particular kinds of touches in particular places, others like erotic stories or watching porn videos.

All kinds of things can start, sustain or increase pleasure, no matter what the size of the penis involved.

Vulva, Labia, clitoris & vaginas

Vulva, labia, clitoris and vaginas are female genitalia. They vary in shape, size and colour as much as penises vary. The vagina is the internal organ and the labia and skin that form the vulva are the visible genitalia on the outside of the body.

Pubic hair may be long or short or removed completely. The vagina is self-cleaning but the rest of the area needs to be washed daily and after exercise and after sex, with a gentle non-irritating soap and rinsed well.

There is a perception that female genitalia look one way, which is the way it is usually portrayed in porn. However, porn is often AI or heavily photoshopped these days, so not in the least bit representative. The colour of the outside and inside of labia vary with a person's skin tone but are different to the skin tone.

Labia are sometimes called lips, they can stick out a little or a lot. Neither is good or bad, beautiful or ugly. It just is. The clitoris is the little nub between the top part of the left and right labia. It gets engorged with blood in the same way that a penis does, getting bigger as pleasured. Many people make the mistake of thinking that the harder you rub a clitoris the nicer it feels. This is not the case and it is very individual. For some people the lightest touch is most pleasurable and for others it is about the directionality of the touch.

Oral sex may involve licking, kissing, sucking or gently biting the clitoris, and/or labia and/or putting the tongue inside the vagina. The taste can vary with what the person eats/drinks as well as the phase of their menstrual cycle if they ovulate. Showering right before sexual activity can prevent anxiety that you are not clean. No matter how clean you are, some people just do not like the texture or taste of giving oral sex to someone with a vagina. Much in the same way that some people just do not like giving oral sex to someone with a penis.

69

Pain during sex

Pain during sex can be as a result of psychological, medical and/or physical discomfort. When sex has previously been painless and there is now pain or discomfort during or just after sex, this should always be checked out by a medical professional. You may want to discuss this with your regular GP/family doctor or at your local sexual health clinic, if there is one near you.

It is always better to get things checked as soon as possible as most causes of pain during or just after sex are treatable with a change of position, change of soap/condom type and/or lubricant type, medication, exercises or other forms of therapy.

Penis pain

Penis pain can be caused by a number of things. If the angle is not quite right when the penis is penetrating a vagina or anus, it can put pressure and strain on that can be quite painful. If this is the case, the individual may be enjoying the sex and focused on that and not notice the pain until after they withdraw OR they may notice it instantly. These are known as physical or mechanical causes of penis pain.

Veronica - *she/her, straight, polyamourous*
My long term partner gets carried away during sex. He likes to change positions frequently during sex for whatever reason. I don't mind as I'm multi

233

orgasmic and so he would usually ask me to move after an orgasm. I can feel his dick in my pussy with quite a lot of sensitivity, so when he is fucking me at a certain angle, which we both enjoy, I just know this is going to hurt him after! I always tell him straight away. Sometimes he'll tweak the angle so it won't hurt after and sometimes he says it is too nice and he doesn't want to stop. Then it hurts after!

Another physical cause of penile pain is friction/rubbing of the penis. If there is not enough lubricant and/or the rubbing is too forceful, it can cause friction burns, which are painful. Interestingly the friction burns may be felt by one or both of the people, rather than always being felt by both. Lube can help prevent friction burns but rough sex is more likely to result in pain than more gentle thrusting.

Other causes of pain can be things like contact dermatitis or allergic reactions, for example to latex condoms or lube. These tend to result in rashes or swelling of the penis in localised areas. Once someone experiences allergic reactions including contact dermatitis they can become more susceptible to these reactions.

Xavier - he/him, bisexual, 30's

I started getting this rash around the top of the shaft of my penis, just below the head in a full ring. My partner and I had stopped living together but were still hooking up. I wasn't using condoms with her as we had agreed a couple of years before to not use them together, but to use them with anyone else we had sex with. When I got the rash, I accused her of giving me an STI and was really quite mean to her. She gently suggested that I was allergic to the soap I was using in the shower as previously she always bought the bathroom products and these were always hypoallergenic. She offered to get a full STI screen as long as I went for a sexual health check up too. The clinic Dr said it was contact dermatitis either from the chemicals at work or the new soap I was using at home. Both our STI screens were clear. I did feel bad that I had accused her, when it was nothing to do with her. But I guess if we had been using condoms too, then I wouldn't have blamed her initially.

Other causes of penile pain include diseases, medical conditions and STIs. STIs that cause pain include: chlamydia, gonorrhoea, genital herpes and syphilis. Urinary tract infections (UTIs) can also cause penile pain, especially if they have occurred due to anal sex without condoms. Antibiotics treat UTIs and some STIs, including chlamydia, gonorrhoea, and syphilis whilst antiviral medications can help reduce or shorten herpes outbreaks.

Prolonged erections can also be extremely painful, and may occur without medications such as Viagra. Urgent medical treatment should be sought for this condition which is known as priapism. Priapism may also occur as a side effects of drugs used to treat erection problems or drugs used to treat depression. Other reasons are

- blood clotting disorders
- mental health disorders
- blood disorders, such as leukemia or sickle cell anaemia
- alcohol use
- illegal drug use
- injury to the penis or spinal cord

If needed, medically drawing blood from the penis can reduce the erection.

Injuring or bending the penis too much can cause significant pain and can cause bleeding inside the penis. Peyronie's disease is an inflammation that causes a thin sheet of scar tissue, called plaque, to form along the upper or lower ridges of the shaft of the penis. This scar tissue forms next to the tissue that becomes hard during an erection, which can result in your penis bending when it's erect, when it did not previously do so. This can be treated medically and/or surgically.

Testicle Pain

Testicles/balls can become painful due to a wide range of things including injuring them! Often, testicle issues cause abdominal or groin pain before pain in the testicle develops. This is why new and unexplained abdominal or groin pain should always be evaluated medically.

Pain in the scrotum/testicles can be the result of serious conditions like testicular torsion or a sexually transmitted infection (STI). Ignoring the pain may cause irreversible damage to the testicles and scrotum. Even kidney stones can cause pain in the testicles!

Call your doctor for an appointment if:

- you feel a lump in your balls/scrotum
- your scrotum is red, warmer to the touch than the surrounding areas, or tender (sore to touch)
- and you develop a fever
- or you've recently been in contact with someone who has the mumps

You should seek emergency medical attention if your testicular pain:

- is sudden or severe
- occurs along with nausea or vomiting
- is caused by an injury that's painful or if swelling occurs after one hour

Vaginal pain

Like penile pain, vaginal pain can occur for a variety of reasons. People can experience vaginal and/or vulval pain. Many women experience vaginal cramping and pain during menstruation, which may be helped with medication, heat and/or sex. However, for some people sex during their period feels uncomfortable and they do not enjoy it.

Pain that is unrelated to your period is likely to be from friction (rough penetrative sex or penetrative sex without enough lubricant), STIs, or a medical condition.

STIs that can cause vaginal pain, itching and burning include:

- Genital herpes
- Gonorrhoea
- chlamydia
- trichomoniasis.

You need to be tested to determine what the cause is and prescribed the appropriate medical treatment.

Yeast infections, often known as thrush, cause swelling, itching and pain, especially during sex or urination. Thrush can be accompanied by a fishy smelling discharge. For susceptible people, vaginal yeast infections can be triggered by antibiotics. Thrush can be treated with natural yoghurt applied using a tampon inserted into the vagina or with over the counter medication.

If you experience painful penetrative vaginal with sensations of rawness, throbbing, burning, stinging and itching over a period of three or more months, this is known as vulvodynia. The pain from this condition is horrible and can make wearing tight clothing painful. It is recommended to wear natural fibres and loose-fitting clothes, and to seek medical treatment. Topical lignocaine can prevent or minimise pain during sex but should not be used without medical guidance.

Vaginismus

Vaginismus is a condition where the vaginal muscles involuntarily contract during attempts at penetration, causing discomfort or preventing penetrative sex altogether.

These contractions may occur not just during attempts at penetrative sex, but also when trying to insert a tampon and even when being touched around the vulva or near the vaginal area.

Someone who experiences vaginismus can still become sexually aroused but the condition can hinder or totally prevent penetration. There should be no shame around this condition, which is treatable.

Vaginismus is classified into 'Primary Vaginismus' when vaginal penetration has never been achieved and 'Secondary Vaginismus' when vaginal penetration was possible before but is no longer due to factors like gynaecologic surgery, trauma, or radiation or post-menopause.

Post-menopause vaginismus is due to decreased vaginal lubrication and elasticity caused by lower estrogen levels.

The exact cause of vaginismus is not always clear but may be associated with past sexual abuse or trauma, previous painful intercourse and/or psychological factors. Sometimes, no direct cause can be identified.

The main symptom of vaginismus is involuntary tightening of the vaginal muscles, making penetration difficult or impossible. Severity varies among individuals. Additional symptoms may include fear of penetration and reduced sexual desire related to it. Women with vaginismus often experience burning or stinging pain with vaginal insertion.

Despite vaginismus, women can still enjoy sexual pleasure, have orgasms, and engage in activities like oral sex, massage, or masturbation that do not involve penetration.

Diagnosis typically begins with discussing symptoms and medical history, including any past trauma or abuse. A pelvic exam is usually necessary, though some women may feel anxious about it. Doctors can adapt the exam for comfort, such as using different positions or allowing the patient to observe using a mirror. They will gently look for signs of infection or scarring.

If vaginismus is suspected, the exam aims to confirm that there is no physical cause for the vaginal muscle contractions. Treatment usually includes education, counselling, and pelvic floor exercises and vaginal dilators that are designed to very slowly stretch the muscles to allow penetration to take place without pain. Women who have successfully completed treatment have reported that they are ale to enjoy penetrative sex.

Other causes of pain in the vagina during sexual intercourse are cysts, pelvic inflammatory disease, or vaginal atrophy. Bartholin glands are situated at the vaginal opening and are responsible for vaginal lubrication. Occasionally they can become blocked, causing a Bartholin's cysts. These may come and go unnoticed, or they may become pus filled and painful requiring treatment. The resultant pain may be present whether you're sitting, walking or having sex. Sitting in a warm bath or pouring lukewarm salt water over the cysts may ease your discomfort. If the pain or swelling persists, seek medical evaluation as you may need surgical drainage or antibiotics.

Endometriosis is the leading cause of pelvic pain, which can then lead to vaginal and even vulval pain. The pain from endometriosis is usually worse during menstruation. Endometriosis often requires surgery and can be completely eradicated with a full hysterectomy.

70

Sexual Health

The main types of sexually transmitted infections are listed below, along with symptoms and treatments.

Herpes HSV1 & HSV2

Genital herpes is caused by the herpes simplex virus (HSV1 or HSV2). While HSV1 typically affects the mouth area, it can also manifest on the genitals, whereas HSV2 primarily affects the genital region. It's estimated that approximately 12% of adults carry the herpes simplex virus, with around 80% of those infected unaware of their status due to asymptomatic cases. The onset of symptoms after infection can vary widely, from weeks to years, or may never manifest.

The herpes simplex virus spreads through skin-to-skin contact, making transmission possible during vaginal, oral, or anal sex. Oral herpes (cold sores) can transmit genital herpes during oral sex. Pregnant women with genital herpes should inform their healthcare provider as there's a rare risk of transmitting the infection to the baby during childbirth, potentially leading to complications.

Symptoms of genital herpes can include flu-like symptoms such as headaches, back pain, and enlarged groin glands. It may also present with small blisters around the genital area that rupture into painful ulcers, along with redness, itching, or a distinct rash. Pain and swelling in the genital region, along with discomfort during urination, can occur.

Women infected with genital herpes may experience similar symptoms as men, including flu-like symptoms, painful ulcers, itching, redness, and discomfort during urination.

There is no cure for genital herpes, but treatment aims to manage symptoms and reduce outbreaks. Approaches include salt baths, ice packs on affected areas, pain relievers like paracetamol, and antiviral medications such as acyclovir, famciclovir, or valaciclovir. These medications are most effective when taken at the onset of symptoms. It's important to note that topical antivirals used for cold sores are not suitable for genital herpes.

Chlamydia

Chlamydia is a common sexually transmitted infection caused by the bacterium Chlamydia trachomatis. It can affect individuals of all ages but is most prevalent among those under 25. Chlamydia can be asymptomatic but, if untreated, may lead to complications like pelvic inflammatory disease (PID).

Chlamydia spreads through unprotected vaginal or anal sex with an infected individual. In men, it primarily affects the urethra and may extend to the epididymis. In women, it can infect the cervix and progress to the uterus and fallopian tubes, potentially causing PID, chronic pelvic pain, or infertility. Pregnant women with chlamydia can pass the infection to their newborn during childbirth, resulting in eye or lung infections.

Men with chlamydia may experience symptoms such as penile discharge, painful urination, or swollen testicles.

Most women infected with chlamydia do not exhibit symptoms. When symptoms occur, they may include abnormal vaginal discharge, burning sensation during urination, pain during sexual intercourse, abnormal bleeding, or lower abdominal pain.

Early detection allows for effective treatment with antibiotics, usually a single dose. Complications like PID may require longer antibiotic courses. Partners should be tested and treated to prevent re-infection.

Syphilis

Syphilis is a sexually transmitted infection caused by the bacterium Treponema pallidum. It progresses through several stages and can lead to severe complications if untreated. Syphilis spreads through direct skin-to-skin contact during sexual activity, including oral, vaginal, or anal sex. It can also pass from a pregnant woman to her foetus.

Syphilis presents in three stages. In the initial stage (primary syphilis), a painless sore (chancre) appears on the genitals, anus, or mouth. In the secondary stage, a rash may appear on the palms or soles, along with flu-like symptoms. If untreated, syphilis can progress to the tertiary stage, affecting organs such as the brain and heart.

Penicillin is the primary treatment for syphilis at all stages. Early detection and treatment are crucial to prevent complications.

Gonorrhoea

Gonorrhoea is caused by the bacterium Neisseria gonorrhoeae and primarily affects the genital area, though it can also involve the throat or anus. Gonorrhoea spreads through unprotected vaginal, oral, or anal sex.

Men with gonorrhoea may experience painful urination, penile discharge, or swollen testicles.

Many women with gonorrhoea are asymptomatic. Symptoms, when present, may include abnormal vaginal discharge, pain during urination, or bleeding between periods.

Gonorrhoea is treated with antibiotics. However, resistant strains are emerging, necessitating careful treatment selection based on antibiotic susceptibility testing.

Scabies

Scabies is a skin infestation caused by the Sarcoptes scabiei mite, characterized by intense itching and skin burrows. Scabies spreads through prolonged skin-to-skin contact, including sexual activity. It can also transmit indirectly through contaminated bedding or clothing.

Symptoms include severe itching (often worse at night), visible skin burrows, and a rash of bumps or blisters.

Treatment involves topical creams or lotions to kill the mites. All close contacts should also be treated to prevent reinfestation.

Pubic Lice (Crabs)

Pubic lice are parasitic insects (Phthirus pubis) that infest pubic hair and can cause itching and irritation. Pubic lice spread through direct skin-to-skin contact, including sexual activity, or indirectly through shared bedding or clothing.

Symptoms include itching in the affected area, visible lice or eggs (nits) in pubic hair, and sometimes sores from scratching.

Topical creams or lotions containing permethrin are used to eradicate pubic lice. Infested clothing and bedding should be washed thoroughly.

Hepatitis

Hepatitis refers to liver inflammation caused by hepatitis viruses (A, B, C). Hepatitis B and C can become chronic, leading to severe liver damage or cancer. Hepatitis B spreads through blood, vaginal fluid, or semen, typically through unprotected sex, sharing needles, or from mother to baby during childbirth.

Symptoms of acute hepatitis B include fever, fatigue, nausea, abdominal pain, joint pain, and jaundice. Chronic infection can lead to long-term liver disease or cancer.

Most adults clear acute hepatitis B on their own, but chronic cases may require antiviral medications to manage the infection and prevent complications. Vaccines are useful to provide immunity, although some vaccinated people can lose immunity and require booster shots.

HIV and AIDS

HIV weakens the immune system and can progress to AIDS (acquired immune deficiency syndrome) if untreated. HIV spreads through unprotected sex, sharing needles, or from mother to child during childbirth or breastfeeding.

Early HIV symptoms can mimic flu-like illnesses and may include fever, swollen lymph nodes, rash, fatigue, and weight loss. Untreated HIV can progress to AIDS, where the immune system is severely compromised, leading to opportunistic infections and cancers.

There's no cure for HIV/AIDS, but antiretroviral therapy (ART) can control the virus, allowing people with HIV to live healthy lives. Early diagnosis and treatment are critical. People who are HIV+ can live long healthy lives with medication.

Using condoms consistently and correctly during sexual activity can significantly reduce the risk of contracting STIs. Regular 3-12 monthly sexual health check-ups, including screenings for STIs, are recommended for sexually active individuals to detect infections early and prevent complications.

Please note the only contraception that is 100% effective is no penis in vagina. To prevent conception always use both condoms (or a vasectomy) and female birth control (or hysterectomy or tubal ligation). The pull out method is notoriously ineffective.

71

3 Minute Game (adapted)

This is a 3-minute game to practice consensual and intentional touch. It was initially drawn up by Harry Faddis and adapted by Betty Martin, who incorporated it into her wheel of consent work.

3 minutes might be too difficult if you have sensory issues or are still healing from trauma. For trauma survivors, only use or adapt this following discussion with your personal therapist of counsellor. You may choose to start off by playing for 10-30 seconds at a time and that is fine too.

The game simply consists of one person asking the other; "How would *you like me to touch you* for 3 minutes? (or the pre-agreed timeframe)". Then the 2nd question or offer is "How would *you like to touch me* for 3 minutes? (or the pre-agreed timeframe).

The idea behind this game is two-fold;

Firstly, to learn what kinds of touches where you like to receive and/or give.

Secondly, to explore different types and levels of consensually giving and receiving.

The person giving the touch may be **serving** the recipient by **doing a particular type of touch that they know will give the recipient pleasure.** OR the person giving the touch may be **taking** pleasure by **doing a particular type of touch that they know will give themselves pleasure.**

The person receiving the touch may be **allowing** the touch knowing that **it will give the person touching, pleasure.** OR they may be **accepting** of the touch as **pleasurable for the recipient of the touch.**

This is often represented in a diagram like the one below:

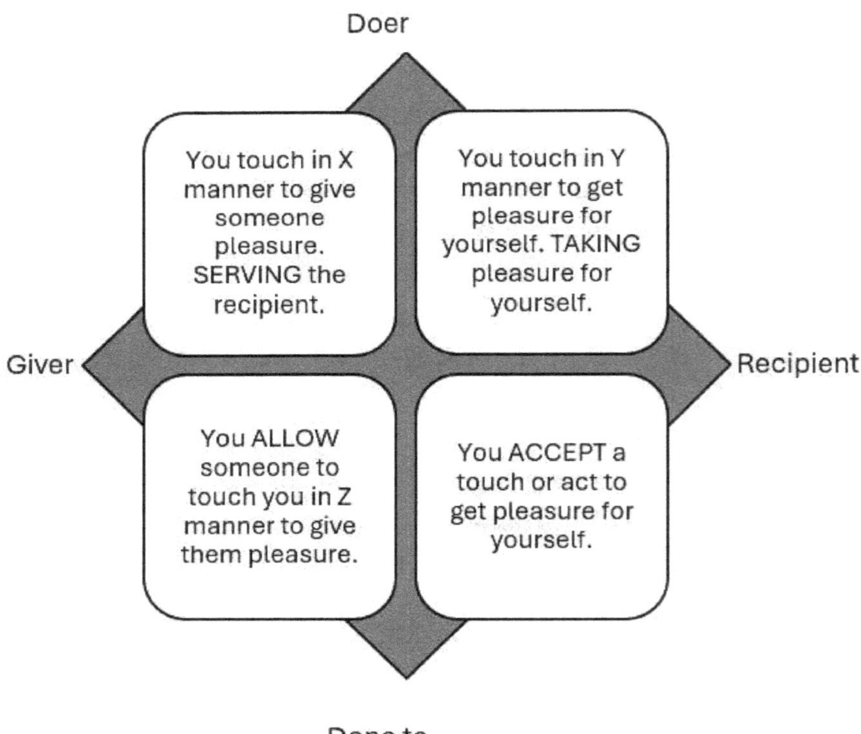

The idea is to gently and safely explore serving, taking, allowing and accepting. Many people are highly uncomfortable accepting pleasure, whilst some prefer to take than to serve, not understanding the emotional and sexual power in served in giving pleasure to an intimate partner.

None of these attributes are inherently bad, however healthy relationships need to have more serving and accepting that taking and allowing.

F*ck, Really? Sexploits

This book aims to educate and entertain, so that people can identify and explore their sexual fantasies and desires without judgement, in their heads before going out into the 'real world'. Learning what you like, might like, won't like and how to do the things you like safely, sanely and with consent.

www.ingramcontent.com/pod-product-compliance
Lightning Source LLC
Chambersburg PA
CBHW071434200726
48294CB00002B/636